A

Collection

of

Small Endings

A

Collection

of

Small Endings

By JC Rock

*The end isn't the last word. It's just the moment life
turns the page.*

A Collection of Small Endings

© 2025 JC Rock Published by Erendi Publishing

First print edition: 2025

ISBN: 978-1-950903-29-0

Edited and designed by Erendi Publishing

www.erendi.com

Printed in the United States of America

ERENDI
PUBLISHING

Carolina

"The road remembers more than it forgets."

Chapter One
The Seventh Visit

Death don't knock on your door if he
knows the way in.

Cicadas sang in the heat of the day and Carolina stood there, eyes closed, basking in the afternoon sun. In all the world there wasn't a better sound than that, not even a baby's laugh. That was a close second, though.

The old black woman hefted up the shoulder pole and set it in place, empty buckets swinging on each end. She was getting too old for this, but if she wanted to wash up after dinner, then she had to make a visit to the old well. Her daughter, Mina, had tried on more than one occasion to have running water brought into her old cabin, but Carolina refused. Been doin' it this way my whole life, too old to change things up now. Besides, the exercise would do her some good.

Carolina cursed her stiff knee and started the walk down the path. She grumbled under her breath; how many pairs of shoes had she worn out walking this path?

Truth be known, she would love to have some running water, or perhaps just a well that was closer to the cabin. She just never could justify the cost. Carolina was a few days shy of her hundredth birthday, no sense changing things around now.

Carolina hummed a few bars of "The Old Rugged Cross" as she ambled down the path. She wasn't what anyone would call a good Christian woman. The only time she ever set foot in a church was on her wedding day, and that was only because her mother-in-law had insisted they have a church wedding. She liked the music on the radio, though, and this far out in the swamp about the only thing her old Motorola would pick up was the religious station from out of Shreveport.

She was the local witch woman, a healer. It had always been a source of pride for her and her family. For nearly 75 years Carolina had treated the people of the surrounding area. She cured the people's ails, delivered their babies, and even said the final words over them that needed it.

Something rustled in the bushes ahead of her and she stopped mid-stride, buckets swinging at the end of the pole. She stilled her off-tune humming and listened. Carolina wasn't afraid of anything in the swamp, she knew everything there was to know about it after the life she had led, but she was cautious. She might have been able to outrun a gator in her youth, but she was not as fast as she once was.

Carolina strained her hearing, but the sound didn't repeat itself. She walked on, enjoying the light breeze that had picked up. "Storm comin' in. Yes indeed," she said in a raspy voice. This far out in the swamp she spent a lot of time talking to herself.

The well-worn trail curled around the knees of an old cypress tree, and Carolina paused and looked up, smiling. Dappled sunlight shone down through the thick canopy, lighting up dozens of charms hung from its boughs. Each one of them was hung by her. I might be a bit slower now, but I can still shimmy myself up a tree when I need to. She squinted until she caught sight of the charm she placed for her husband on their wedding day. She nodded and moved on.

After several more minutes the clearing came into sight, with the old well at its center. Once Carolina reached the well, she plopped the buckets down on the ground, then sat down heavily on the bench beside it. The bench had been a gift from her daughter. If she wasn't going to allow running water in her house, she should at least have a bench to rest on. Carolina had to admit she enjoyed sitting on the bench and watching the wind blow through the leaves.

Carolina felt unsettled today though; something didn't quite feel right to her and she couldn't place her finger on what it was. Carolina was acutely aware of all of her different aches and pains and feels. This was something else. Her mind was unsettled, something she hadn't felt for a long time. She froze, knowing what was wrong. She'd almost forgotten the time was coming.

"Is that you?" she called out, her voice clear and powerful. "I know'ed you be back. Has it really been seven years?" Carolina thought back. By her reckoning she had been 93 the last time the dog came for her. Right on time, sort of.

"You're a few days early," she said to the breeze. "My birthday ain't for a few more days. Go home you black devil, I ain't quite done."

Carolina's dark eyes scanned the deepening pools of shadow around the clearing. The cicadas and birds had stopped their songs. Even the breeze seemed to whisper reverently as it tickled the hairs on her arms. Then she saw them: a pair of red eyes glowing in the gloom across the clearing. They blinked slowly at her, watching and waiting. "There you be. Come on out you devil, let me lay eyes on you. My poor old peepers ain't what they used to be. Come into the sun." Carolina straightened the fabric of her skirt where it laid in her lap, making herself presentable for an old acquaintance.

The eyes watching her winked out and Carolina felt a chill rush up her spine. Her mother used to say when you felt like that then a rabbit was running over your grave. Black smoke swirled around the clearing in tiny wisps that seemed to rise up from the very ground itself. She'd seen it happen dozens of times in her life, but it never ceased to send a chill through her bones. It was like the black dog rose from the very depths of hell.

The smoke swirled together across the clearing from her. More and more wisps of smoke coalesced until a faint shape appeared. A moment later the black dog stood there watching her.

Carolina smiled in spite of herself, her yellowed teeth in stark contrast to her dark skin. The dog was a portent of death, but over the years it had almost become a companion of sorts. Ever since she was a little girl the black dog had been there.

The dog became almost solid and sat down on its hindquarters. It was a huge dog, bigger than any others Carolina had ever seen. She'd read about dire wolves that roamed in olden times and this dog reminded her of those stories. It sat there panting at her, its tongue hanging out, seeming to smile at her like it was waiting for her to throw a ball for it to chase. It cocked its head questioningly.

"I told you, it ain't time."

Thunder rumbled across the swamp and dark clouds gathered overhead, stealing the warmth of the sunshine from her old bones. Carolina rose and grabbed one of the buckets, keeping an eye on the dog. If she was going to make it back home before the storm hit, she better get going.

The dog watched as Carolina hooked the bucket up to the rope and dropped it down the well. The crank turned freely and then a splash echoed up from below. Carolina grunted with the effort of turning the crank until the bucket appeared over the edge. She placed the bucket on the lip of the well and unhooked it, then filled the second bucket the same way.

Lightning flashed across the sky and Carolina jumped. "Gracious," she said to the dog. "Look at the effect you have on me. Makin' an old woman jump like that."

Carolina picked up the shoulder pole and hooked the buckets on. She grunted, lifting the pole into place. "See, not so weak now am I?" she said. "I got things to do, be on your way devil. It ain't time."

Carolina knew the black dog was only tormenting her. It liked to play games. She turned her back to the dog. It took all her courage to put the dog to her back, but she started down the path that would lead her home to her tiny cabin. She walked as quickly as she could, mostly to beat the storm but also to put some distance between her and the dog. Several times along the way she could hear the dog barking, almost laughingly, mocking her.

Midway through her walk back, she felt something like a weight being lifted from her shoulders, a lightening of her soul. For now the dog had left her alone, but he would be back. She had two more days before the dog would want her to join him. Until then, she knew, he was going to give her gentle reminders of what he was going to want. This was the seventh time he had come for her. Carolina wondered if she would be able to do what he wanted one more time. Should she even try? She knew the answer before she even asked the question. Too many people depended on her. She had to do what she had to do.

The walk back home helped lift her spirits. Being out there with Mother Nature had a calming effect on her, and ever since she was young, the daily walks out to the well had been a much-needed break in her day. When nothing else in the world was going right, a walk in the trees would help fix most things.

Her cabin came into sight, welcoming her. The dark clouds pushed tight across the sky but still a stray beam of light shone down on the covered porch, highlighting the faded white paint. It was a simple three-room cabin with kitchen, bed-room, and living room, with a fireplace for cooking and other things. She had electric power, but never liked the look of the drooping power lines connected to the side of the cabin and wished she could just do away with them. She didn't think the power was necessary, but it had been a concession to her daughter. The girl was such a fuss bucket, always worrying about things.

Carolina passed the small outhouse and stepped onto the first step leading up to the porch. For the second time that day, a stray noise made her freeze, head cocked to the side and lis-tening. It was a sound she hadn't heard in nearly 50 years. Someone sat in her husband's old hardwood rocker, some-thing that was strictly forbidden. Not even she enjoyed the pleasure, though that was more out of guilt.

Carolina climbed the remaining steps and put the buckets and pole down on the porch. She looked at the front door of the house but it appeared to be just how she left it. There was no lock on the door, but in all her years of living in the swamp one had never been needed. She was born in that cabin, had lived her whole life in it, and if the good spirits were willing, then she would spend her last moments in it as well. She'd always felt safe in it.

She raised a hand to touch the pentacle on the front door that she had made out of woven grapevines. It helped ward off evil spirits from the swamp and was usually all the protection she needed. For anything a bit more substantial she had a twelve-gauge shotgun under her mattress, but she hadn't touched that in years. She peered in through the dirty glass windows, making a mental note to wash them next chance she got. From this angle she couldn't see who was sitting in the rocker, but she could still hear the runners rocking back and forth, thumping on the edge of the braided rug in the living room.

Carolina pushed the door open and the smell hit her. She nearly dropped to her knees, recognizing it immediately. She only knew one person who smoked a pipe with tobacco that smelled like that. She took a few steps, almost daring not to look. Her heart skipped a beat when she finally turned her eyes toward the chair and its occupant.

"Darrell?" Carolina couldn't keep the surprise from her voice. Of all the people that could show up, she never expected it to be him. After all, he had been dead for nearly 50 years.

"Hi, Chicken."

Her face flushed when he used his old nickname for her. "What you be doin' here? No offense, but you dead."

Darrell pulled the pipe from his mouth and stopped rocking. He smiled at her and his whole face squished up. She always thought he looked like a prune when he did that.

"Oh, no one knows that better'n me. 'Cept maybe you."

Carolina felt a small pang of guilt but she let it pass quickly.

She was over that a long time ago. She shuffled across the room to turn on the lamp, chasing away the darkness. When she turned to sit in her own chair, Darrell was still there, puffing away on that infernal pipe, his face lit by the glow of it.

"I've made my peace with that," she said.

"No doubt, no doubt. You always were made of rubber. Bad stuff just bounces right off you like it was nothing." His voice turned sullen, "The good stuff, too. You shrug your shoulders and the world falls away like it was nothing. You may live on this world, but you ain't a part of it."

Carolina eyed him critically, amazed he looked exactly the same now as he did back then. "Best way to be. Someone like me sees a lot of pain, a lot of death."

Darrell nodded. "Truth. But you're not supposed to cause it."

Darrell fell silent, puffing on his pipe once again. Carolina remembered how he was. He could sit for hours with his pipe, staring out the window like he was solving all the world's problems in his mind. Carolina chuckled to herself; the only problem he ever solved was how to get out of doing the hard work that needed doing. She loved him though, still did if she thought about it. Most of the time it seemed she just didn't like him too much, and that was more important to her.

"Why are you here, Darrell?"

Darrell turned his one blue eye on her. It was one of the first things she noticed about him when they met. He had one blue eye and one black eye. "You seen the black dog?"

So that was it. The dog still tormented her by sending Darrell. Dredging up the past to make her miserable.

"I have. Reckon you know that, though. It ain't time yet."

Carolina grabbed her knitting from the table beside her. She didn't like to knit, but sometimes it helped ease her mind so she could think.

"Don't matter if it's time or not. This time is different. Six times he come for you, and six times you put him off. This time he gonna ask for something special."

Carolina humphed. The dog always wanted something special as far as she was concerned. After all, what was more special than a life?

"What are you making?" Darrell pointed at the knitting with the mouthpiece of his pipe.

Carolina looked down at her knitting, a colorful but shapeless mess. She never really accomplished making anything, just threw stitches together. "Tea cozy?" she quipped.

Darrell laughed and Carolina remembered how sweet a sound it was.

"Shoot woman, I ain't never seen you drink tea. Whiskey maybe."

Carolina smiled then. That was supposed to be her little secret. She'd gotten into the habit of drinking a small glass of bourbon before bed. But she hadn't started that until after Darrell died.

"You been watching me?"

It was Darrell's turn to shrug. "From time to time. Gotta keep tabs on my woman. You always had a fine backside."

Carolina flushed. Darrell was always a bit of a rogue when it came to women, with a roaming eye and grabby hands. It made what she had to do to him easier. That's what she told herself, anyway.

The storm outside gathered intensity and Carolina could see the trees bending over in the wind. It was a night just like this one that the dog had come for her that first time. The memory of that night came up unbidden. Carolina suspected that might have had something to do with seeing the dog earlier.

Chapter Two
Smoke and Memory

Some ghosts wear skin and smile like they never left.

Carolina paced nervously across the porch, back and forth, over and over. A storm was rising up and if the pain in her knee was any indication, then it was going to be a doozy. Her eyes scanned the water again for any sign of Darrell. He'd been out fishing all day and should have been home hours ago. She had been feeling poorly all day and having him out on the water in these conditions wasn't helping her anxiety at all. She ought to just let the swamp take him, curse his hide. Never around when she needed him.

Lightning flashed, throwing shadows all around and making her jump. Normally she loved storms. The power of them made her feel so alive, yet this one felt ominous somehow, almost like she could sense evil lurking in the shadows. When she was younger she would stand out in them with arms spread wide, almost daring the spirits to strike her down. Over the years she had learned a bit of caution At least she had learned not to tempt the spirits but so much.

Something caught her eye, something at the edge of the clearing where her husband pulled the boat up out of the water. Darrell? Shadows seemed to swirl around as she strained to see through the rain and the gloom. Her uneasy feelings grew.

Lightning flashed again and she saw clear what it was: a great black dog standing there in the rain. Carolina gasped when she realized what it was. The dog stared at her, red eyes blazing like the fires of hell in the gloom.

Carolina knew the black dog, knew the legend. She'd seen the dog before, perhaps a dozen times. He always came to usher those lost souls to their new homes. As the local witch woman, Carolina had been there to see quite a few people make that final journey. Very few people could see the dog, and at this moment Carolina wished she couldn't.

Why was the dog here now? Her mind raced with possibilities. She settled on one. Darrell! Something had happened to him out on the water and the dog was there to take him away from her. That had to be it. That fool old man got himself in trouble for the last time.

Carolina sat down on the top step, buried her face in her hands. Lightning flashed again as she felt a pain in her chest, like a vise closing down on her inch by inch. She bent over as it grew hard for her to breathe. Was she having a panic attack? She'd seen other people have them, had treated her fair share. No, this was something more.

Her vision blurred and she could hear her heart beating heavily in her ears.

The dog moved closer, watching her with head cocked in the rain.

"You be here for me?" Carolina asked. She already knew the answer.

Laughter echoed around her.

"It's too soon. Too many people depend on me, need me." Pain coursed through her chest.

"The widow Parsons," Carolina managed to get out. "She got

the pairs in her head only I can stop. And the others…"

It hurt to draw even the smallest of breaths when all she needed to do was gasp. Light flashed in her vision and she fell backward, thumping her head on the porch floor. It can't end like this, she thought.

Carolina turned her head and saw the dog standing there on the porch beside her. It seemed to be smiling at her, pleased with itself that it was taking her. It looked hungry.

"There has to be something I can do," she managed to gasp out the words. "Just name your price and I will do it. Anything. We can make some kinda deal, can't we?"

The dog sat down on its haunches and stared at her, seeming to consider her words. To Carolina it felt like the dog was looking right down into her soul, judging her past.

"Just let me stay a bit longer."

The dog cocked its head. Carolina blinked away the rain in her eyes. The dog turned to wispy smoke in front of her and a pair of legs appeared.

"What's wrong, Chicken? Come on, let's get you out of this rain."

Carolina felt his strong hands under her, easily lifting her into his arms and carrying her into the cabin. She was aware of his footsteps echoing through the cabin and then she was laid on her bed.

"What can I do? Tell me what you need." Darrell's voice was calm, though it was easy to see from his face he was panicked.

Carolina tried to think through the pain. She was pretty sure she was having a heart attack. She knew the powders she would need, and even had some mixed up already.

"Blue bottle," she managed to gasp out. "Top… top shelf, right side."

She heard him stomp into the kitchen where her potions were kept. Fire lanced across her chest. Carolina tried to sit up, but she was far too weak. Not even when she heard her bottles being shuffled around and dropped could she gather the strength. Those bottles were her livelihood, and hearing them break and crushed underfoot hurt almost as much as her chest did.

Darrell came back in after a moment, and with the right bottle, she noted. He also had a glass of water.

Carolina pointed at the blue bottle with two fingers, then at the glass and made a stirring motion.

Darrell had watched her enough over the years to understand what she needed. He put two pinches of the powder in the water and stirred it with his finger. He helped her sit up and drink down the bitter concoction. She choked down the whole glass, praying to the good spirits and even the black dog itself to give her more time. The community needed her expertise, along with her powders and potions. Her vision grew dim. Somewhere at the edge of her hearing she heard the laughing howl of the black dog. She was dying and the spirits had ignored her request. She closed her eyes to give herself up to the dog.

Chapter Three

Storm Warning

The dog always comes in the rain—like
sorrow dressed for travel.

The first thing she became aware of was a bright light. She recognized the smell of her cabin, the heavy quilt laying on top of her. She was hot so she pushed away the covers and opened her eyes.

Sunlight streamed in through the small window over her bed. Carolina was surprised she was still alive. She'd obviously slept through the night. She sat up and swung her legs over the side of the bed. It felt like she had been asleep for a week, but otherwise she felt fine, strong in fact. The bed springs creaked under her when she moved.

She heard movement and looked up to see Darrell's body blocking the small doorway.

"Carolina?" he almost never called her that. Usually it was only when he was angry with her, or worried. "Don't get up, I will get you some water."

Carolina opened her mouth to speak but couldn't get the words past the cotton in her mouth. She couldn't get any words out until she drank half the water Darrell returned with. "How long?"

"Been two days, laying there. Camilla has been here, checking on you. She told me what herbs to give you, while you was sleeping. Mixed it up with water and got you to take little sips."

Carolina nodded, that would explain the taste of comfrey at the back of her throat. "She means well, she ain't trained, though."

"And whose fault is that," Darrell asked. "She's willing."

"She ain't got the feel though, the intuition needed. You can't just be a witch woman. It's something you're born with, or ain't." Carolina sighed. She and Darrell had had this conversation a dozen times or more, usually ending in an argument with Darrell stomping out the house and disappearing for a few days.

"If you ask me, you ain't trained her so you can make yourself more important. You're the only witch woman for miles and miles in any direction. Since Abigail died, you might be the only one in the whole swamp."

"Nobody asked you, old man." There was truth in his words, but she tried to ignore them. It felt nice to be needed the way she was. Darrell didn't understand that, probably never would.

Darrell shuffled off to the living room and Carolina heard his rocker start to creak. Seconds later the smell of his pipe wafted in.

Chapter Four

The Cost of Borrowed Time

Every breath you borrow, you pay back
with interest.

"I will just get my own food, shall I?" She said it out loud, but not loud enough for Darrell to hear. She didn't want a fight today. They had been fighting too much recently.

Carolina stood, a bit unsteadily at first, but quickly found her balance. She shuffled to the kitchen and stood at the counter, looking out the window. An involuntary gasp escaped her lips when she saw the dog sitting in Darrell's small skiff. She knew what it meant.

"You brung Darrell to me. I asked for more time and you brought him back out the swamp to help me."

The dog stared at her through the window. Small wisps of smoke circled around the dog in the sunlight.

"I know there's a price for me bein' here. What is it? I know it wasn't done out of the goodness of whatever black thing you have for a heart."

A small bottle wiggled on a high shelf and Carolina reached to pull it down. It was a poison, a potion she made to help end the suffering of those she could no longer help. She stared at the bottle, somehow knowing what it meant. "You need a life, in exchange for the one you gave back to me."

The dog didn't move, but she knew that is what it wanted. She didn't know how she knew, but she did just the same. "And if I refuse?"

As if in answer, a sharp pain raced across her chest until she couldn't even draw breath.

"Okay, okay. Message received," she managed to get out. "Who is it to be then?"

Pipe smoke drifted by in a big cloud at that moment. "Chicken, who you talking to?"

Carolina felt the blood drain from her face. She knew enough about signs to know what the dog wanted. "Just rattling off one of my lists, you know how I do."

She looked out at the dog, wondering how it could ask such a thing of her. Could she even bring herself to do such a thing? She'd ended the lives of them that were suffering, would it be so different?

The pain in her chest increased. If she let it go too long she would surely succumb to the pain. The tea kettle beside her whistled loudly, making her jump nearly out of her skin. Who put that kettle on? She grabbed the kettle by the handle and pulled it off the stove.

"You gonna bring me that tea or what," Darrell asked from the other room.

Had she put the kettle on? She didn't remember doing it. It didn't matter, though. She knew what was required of her, and the dog had made sure she knew what it was. The thought came again: could she even do it? Was her life worth his? What was he anyway besides a womanizing slacker, dodging work in all its forms unless it was absolutely necessary?

Carolina, however, was an important member of the community. Who would take care of everyone if she were gone? She steeled herself and poured some tea into Darrell's cup, along with a few drops of the poison.

Carolina did well to keep her hands from shaking as she handed him the cup.

* * *

Carolina locked herself away for days after Darrell died. Everyone thought it was because she was grieving. Even now she could still remember the screams from him as the dog came to drag away his soul She couldn't miss the accusations in his screams as the dog took him away. She had never seen anyone fight so hard to stay. The more he fought, the worse the agony of his passing became. She vowed at that moment that she would do whatever it took to make sure the dog never took her away like that. She thought that the dog would leave her alone after that, but every seven years he came for her. And each time the dog offered up a proxy in place of her, to die by her hands.

After Darrell, the dog was content to name the sick and infirm, and that made it easier for her. It became easy for her to justify her actions. Those she sacrificed had little life left to live, or had a life that promised to be one of pain and suffering, one of being a constant burden. Over the years she even managed to ease her guilt over what she did to Darrell. The good spirits hadn't abandoned her, so she must have done the right thing.

The smell of pipe smoke drew Carolina out of her reverie. Darrell still sat, staring at her. His lips pursed when he puffed at the pipe. "Where did you go just now? You had that far-away look."

Carolina wasn't sure she could deal with him anymore this night. "Leave me be old man, I got things to suss out."

"Old man? By my reckoning you're quite a bit older than me."

"You know what I mean."

Darrell nodded. "I got things to do myself."

"Pssh, things to do. You been bone idle your whole life. Don't think things would be any different now you dead and gone."

Darrell stood and pointed the stem of his pipe at her. "You know, things weren't always as bad as what you seem to remember. Time has a way of playing with memories. Maybe you oughta sit down and think on that for a bit. I'll be back soon. The dog has plans for you."

Carolina watched as Darrell's body began to drift apart, becoming wisps of smoke just like the dog itself. Darrell's sad smiled lingered a moment longer, and then even that was gone. The smoke drifted away into nothingness, leaving Carolina standing alone in the middle of the living room with nothing but the lingering smell of pipe smoke. She wrung her hands together, not looking forward to his return. She didn't need any reminders of the things she had done to stay alive. She had a shelf full of things for that.

Was Darrell right? Had she convinced herself that things were so bad back then to make it easier to accept what she had done? Maybe her own selfishness and fear of death made her do what she did.

Carolina shuffled into the small kitchen. The events of the day had worn her out. At the moment she just wanted to have a glass of bourbon and go to bed. Scratch that, she thought, make it a double.

She stood leaning against the counter, looking at the storm that raged outside. Lightning flashed and Carolina dropped the glass she had just filled. The black dog stood out there, surrounded by the ghostly shell of Darrell's boat.

From the time she had killed Darrell, till now, she hadn't been able to bring herself to do anything with the boat. Like the rocker in the other room, Carolina never let anyone touch the boat, not even when a man kept offering her more and more money for it.

Each day for the last 42 years she had stood at that same window and stared out at the boat. Now it was little more than bits of rotted wood, nearly covered by saw-grass and briars. It was also a daily reminder of what she had done. Was that why she kept it, to remind herself? Carolina wondered if it was guilt that brought her to the window day after day.

The dog's eyes winked in the gloom. Carolina felt a twinge in her chest. She knew that pain very well. She reached for the blue bottle that held the powders, then paused. She could let it all end here, let the dog take her. No more victims, no more guilt. And no more justifications.

Carolina's chest tightened even more. She held her breath, pushing away the pain. It would be easy enough, she could even help the process along and take away the pain. But no, she wasn't ready. She still had things to do. And she was scared. Carolina grabbed the blue bottle off its shelf and added a few pinches to a glass of water. She waited for the spasm to pass, then downed the drink.

The black dog howled somewhere out in the swamp. It sounded almost sad somehow, like it wanted Carolina to let go.

Carolina clenched her teeth together, waiting until the pain in her chest subsided. Her glare remained fixed out the window until the powder took full effect. Once the spasm was gone, Carolina glanced at the framed picture sitting on the counter. Five generations of women in her family, from her, all the way down to little Myca. Her great-great-granddaughter was only five, but already showed great potential as a witch woman. If only Carolina had the time to fully train her.

Carolina had already started training the young girl, and she proved to be smart as a whip, but proper training took years.

"Not today, you devil," Carolina yelled at the window. "I got too much to do; young'uns need me, old'uns too."

Carolina wasn't sure if she could bring herself to kill again. She had to find a way to put off the dog long enough to train little Myca. But how?

"Come on spirits, give old Carolina a little inspiration. If you be there for real, you wouldn't want me killing again, even if it was a mercy."

Carolina froze, a grin on her lips. The dog was an evil spirit, but a spirit nonetheless. If she could cast a spell to keep that particular spirit away, then it could never come for her.

Carolina felt a small glimmer of hope and shuffled into the other room to grab her Gran's old spell books.

Chapter Five

The Ghost of a Life

Memory is a trickster—kind to the dead,
cruel to the living.

Carolina spent most of the next day writing, and then rewriting an old spell she found in one of her Gran's books. She wasn't sure if it would work or not, but she had to try. She had to do something other than sit and wait.

As night started to fall, Carolina walked out to her small pen and grabbed a chicken for the spell. She never did like blood magic, but sometimes it was necessary.

The storm from the night before had blown through quickly, leaving everything smelling fresh and new. Nothing beat the smell of the earth after a heavy rain.

It was a short but squishy walk to her casting circle, a small area she had set aside and had a pentacle made out of stones on the ground. She was winded by the time she got there, and something about the place didn't feel quite right at all. She felt someone's presence, but couldn't see anyone.

Strands of smoke started swirling around the center of the pentacle. The chicken Carolina carried screeched and pecked at her until she couldn't hold it anymore and dropped it.

The smoke swirled faster and faster until it coalesced into a small figure. At first, Carolina thought the dog had returned, but as she watched, a little boy appeared in the center of the pentacle.

The boy was no more than six or seven, with sandy blond hair and a devilish grin on his face. He stood there, blue eyes twinkling in the light of Carolina's lantern. There was something familiar about the boy, something she couldn't quite figure out. Not until the boy squatted in the dirt to play with a small toy car he produced from a pocket.

She knew that metal car, and by extension, the boy. She chided herself for not remembering quicker. He had been the second person the dog demanded she take. Carolina almost gave in to the dog then, she refused to offer up a child. At first. But the boy was ill, his tiny heart failing. She kept from taking him as long as she could but the boy's suffering grew more than she could bear. The same poison she used to stop Darrell's heart took away the boy's pain. And then the dog came for him. Carolina begged the dog to take him easy. And the dog, for his part, agreed.

Carolina walked up to the boy and squatted down beside him, both knees popping loudly. The boy smiled up at the noise, "Don't shoot, Sheriff."

Carolina thought back, stretching her memory. "Your name is Ryan, am I right?"

The boy nodded. "I remember you. You helped my pain go away."

The old woman smiled. "And now? How do you feel now?"

Carolina had to know if what she had done had made a difference. She had ended the boy's suffering, but what about the afterlife? Had her involvement with the black dog changed anything?

The boy shrugged, "We play a lot."

"We?"

"The other kids like me. Lots of kids to play with." Carolina fought the tears at the thought of so many children passing away. She had seen more than her fair share herself. She was at least glad to know that kids could still be kids after they died. Carolina loved children and was glad they could all be together.

Ryan turned his attention back to driving the little car around through the sand, making engine noises with pursed lips.

Carolina noticed the black dog watching them from across the clearing. He seemed to be watching the boy with great interest.

"Shoo! Go home devil." Carolina stood back up and stamped her feet in the dirt, clapping her hands together.

Ryan turned his head to see who she was talking to. He jumped up and squealed.

"Come on Ryan, he won't hurt you none. Not as long as you stay with me." She reached out to grab his shoulder, but he was too fast and slipped through her fingers, heading for the dog.

"Blackie!" the boy yelled.

Ryan ran up to the dog and wrapped his tiny arms around the dog's neck, burying his smiling face in the dog's fur. The dog's tongue hung out happily. For just a moment the dog looked normal to her, just a big shaggy dog getting loves from a child.

The dog turned his eyes on Carolina, silently warning her that time was almost up for her. The dog and boy broke apart in wisps of smoke, drifting off into the night.

Carolina knew the spell wasn't going to work now, besides, she had lost her chicken. She doubted she would see it again. Gator would probably get it in the night, dumb bird. She turned and started the walk back to her cabin.

By the time she got home, she was too wrung out, both physically and emotionally, to do anything. She dropped down on the bed and was asleep before her head even hit the pillow.

Chapter Six

A Deal too Far

What will you give to stay alive? What won't you?

Carolina was up with the sun, just like most mornings. This day, though, was a big one for her in more ways than one. Her family would be out this evening to take her out for a special dinner for her birthday tomorrow. It's not every day someone turns 100.

More importantly, it was the day she was going to have to deal with the dog.

Carolina wiped the grit from her eyes and threw her legs over the edge of the bed, wincing a bit at how cold the floor felt this morning. She wiggled a bit to get things moving and then stood. She was always so stiff in the mornings now. She figured it had to happen at some point.

She stepped into her slippers and shuffled across the floor to head outside to make use of the facilities. A sound caught her ears and she paused. She cocked her head to the side until her hearing cleared. Once she realized what the sound was, her heart thumped a bit harder in her chest.

Carolina went into the kitchen and the sound got louder. Tick. Tick. Tick. Each beat seemed to echo around the tiny space.

The old pocket watch sat propped against the cabinet against the back of a small shelf in the corner. It was her special shelf, with a few very special items on it. These were the things she would save if her cabin ever caught fire.

Carolina picked up the watch, turning it over and over in her hand looking at it. The gold case it came in had been missing for years. She hadn't even touched the watch in years, much less wound it up. Still, from time to time the watch would start ticking of its own accord. Perhaps it had been the previous owner making sure she didn't forget who it came from.

How could Carolina forget? The watch belonged to an old man named Xavier. Carolina always thought it was a funny-sounding name. They had been fast friends from the time he showed up on her porch seeking help. She did all she could to help ease his cancer pain, but when the dog came for her once again, she slipped the man the poison that would do what she needed. It was Xavier's death that made her realize she shouldn't form attachments to those she treated. It hurt her too much to have to do that to someone she was close to.

Carolina put the watch up to her cracked lips and gave it a light kiss, then put it back on the shelf. Her hand brushed against another item and she pulled it down. It was the little metal car that belonged to the boy, Ryan. Carolina let the tears flow at the thought of the boy.

The other items on the shelf all belonged to one of the people she had sent off to the dog. Well, almost all. There was also a small item hidden near the back of the shelf.

Carolina picked it up off the shelf and held it reverently in the palm of her hand. It was a tiny carved dog, made out of dark wood. It was the last thing her Gran had given her before she passed. It had also been the first time she saw the black dog take someone.

Chapter Seven

Inheritance

*Magic don't skip generations—it just waits
for the right hands.*

Her Gran lay in bed, gasping for breath. Carolina could almost hear the woman's breath rattle in her chest. In all her five years she thought she had never seen anything so terrifying as her Gran laying there, but she thought it was important to see it. Why wasn't anyone doing anything? Her mother was a witch woman, why wasn't she helping?

Carolina put her hand on the old woman's arm, almost pulling back from how cold she felt.

The old woman's eyes snapped open at her touch and she looked right at Carolina.

"Come closer child," her voice was ragged and weak. "I need to share an old friend with you."

Carolina climbed up on the bed, sitting close to her Gran. She studied the woman's face, remembering every wrinkle and feature.

"Hold your hand out, dear."

Carolina did as she was told and felt her Gran's cold hand close around hers. When her Gran pulled her hand back, Carolina felt something small in the palm of her hand. She looked at the item and smiled. She'd seen the tiny carved dog before, sitting on a high shelf with other items.

"This was given to me when I was about your age by my Gran.

No one knows how long it has been so, but it has been passed down for generations."

Her Gran tried to say more but was struck by a coughing fit.

Carolina's mother took her hand and pulled her off the bed. "Why won't you help her," Carolina asked her mother.

"She don't want it child, says it's her time. That black dog in your hand. Keep it safe."

Gran's coughing fit eased as Carolina watched. The old woman's breathing became impossibly shallow and then stopped altogether. Everyone in the room fell silent.

There was a howling out in the swamp that grew closer and closer, then stopped. Carolina froze as a giant black dog walked into the room, right through the outside wall. No one else seemed to see anything.

Her Gran's spirit sat up, lined in silver light, leaving the body behind. She reached out and patted the black dog and stood. Her Gran and the dog walked right through the wall and out into the night. Everyone in the room was crying but Carolina. She knew something lay after death, and her Gran was headed there.

Chapter Eight

The Child and the Dog

*Even the Devil can look like a friend when
a child smiles at him.*

Carolina slipped the carved dog into her pocket. On this day she felt it a good idea to keep it close, just in case. She stared out the window at the remains of the old boat. At almost the same instant she smelled the pipe smoke once again.

"Come to torment me again," Carolina asked without turning around. "Or have you come to wish me an early birthday."

"If that makes you happy. I'm pretty sure you know why I'm here, though."

"You be trying to convince me to roll over, to let the dog take me home. I say I still got things to do."

"Do you? Let the young'uns take over. It's time for you to rest." Darrell walked across the room and laid a hand on her shoulder, making her jump. "Is my touch so bad?"

Carolina shrugged. "No, not so bad. Just makes me remember."

"I wish that were true, Chicken. You only ever seem to remember the bad. Why is that? We had more good times than bad."

Carolina pulled away from him and walked to the bedroom. "It suits me that way."

"Hmph. It helps you justify what you did to me, to see me as some kind of monster when you know I ain't. You always been so self-important, so sure everyone couldn't do without you."

Carolina didn't want to hear his words. She hummed away tunelessly, ignoring him. Still, his words stung more than she wanted to admit. She laid out her flowery dress on the bed, fingering the stitching. She didn't wear it often, but this was a special occasion. When she turned around, Darrell was gone. She was almost sad. She had enjoyed their little chats of late, even if his words were hitting a little closer to home than she would have liked.

Carolina realized she still hadn't voided her bladder. She walked out onto the porch, rubbing her hands together against the chill of the morning. The dog was laying in the yard and looked up when she came out. Its tail thumped heavily on the ground when it saw her.

"Happy to see me?" Carolina walked down the steps and started across the yard. She doubled over in pain. It felt like her heart was going to leap from her chest. No! It's too soon.

"Please dog, not yet. I got kinfolk coming. I ain't ready." The dog stood, watching her with burning eyes.

"Fine, I admit it, I'm scared to die. Just scared, that's all. I don't want you to take me. Time and again I seen you take souls. Some went peacefully. Some screamed in terror. What's after this for me, after all I done? Please, I have to know. Can you let me know that much at least?"

The dog watched her silently.

"I reckon not. It ain't for me to know beforehand is it? Give me the name, then. Who is it to be? Who's life must I take today?" the dog looked at her sadly, almost like it didn't want to give the name this time.

The dog walked across the yard and picked up a small yellow ball in its mouth, gently, and walked it back to drop it at Carolina's feet.

"No you don't, devil. Not her. Not my little Myca." Her world crashed in around her. There was no way she could give up her great-great-granddaughter to the dog.

Pain lanced across her chest and she dropped to her knees. The vision of the dog in front of her swam in and out. More time, she needed more time. Her vision faded to black.

Chapter Nine
Midnight's Bargain

*Make it to midnight, and the Devil's got to
wait another day.*

Brightness, so bright it hurt. Carolina opened her eyes slowly and looked around. It took a few moments to focus. She couldn't understand at first what she saw. Her family stood all around her.

"Not dead," she asked. "Not dead yet?"

"Not yet momma, I gave you the powders from the blue bottle like you showed me. You're not going anywhere, not yet."

Carolina felt her daughter's hand cover hers. The brightness eased so she could finally focus. "So you say. I know better. I know it's my time, no more putting it off."

"Don't talk like that momma."

Carolina ignored her. "The dog just wants too much this time."

"What are you talking about momma? The black dog? I remember that old story you used to tell me. Old wives' tale, nothing more."

Carolina sighed. Her daughter had never believed.

Her daughter placed a few more pillows under her back and neck, propping her up.

Carolina looked all around. "Darrell, where is Darrell?"

Her daughter frowned at her. "Momma, daddy's been dead a long time. Come on and rest. You will feel better after you rest some." She shooed everyone out of the bedroom.

Darrell stood leaning against the wall, puffing on his pipe.

"Can you ever forgive me, old man?"

Darrell smiled at her. "Already have. Done that long ago."

Carolina smiled, only for a moment, then remembered. "The dog named my proxy."

Darrell nodded and sat on the edge of the bed. "I know. What are you going to do?"

"What do you mean?"

"It's still your call. Until midnight you can still make your choice"

"No choice at all. No way I can give her to the dog, you know that. It ain't right. She ain't sick. So much potential in that one. She just needs training, that's all." Carolina pleaded into the air. "Please dog, give me more time."

"Rest easy, Chicken. Give in, come spend eternity with me."

"What would you want with an old woman like me?" Darrell crossed the room and grabbed the small mirror from her nightstand, showing her the reflection. "Not so old now."

Carolina studied herself in the mirror. She looked 20 again; so beautiful, so alive. The silver was gone from her hair, the age in her eyes gone as well. She nodded, her choice had already been made. "So be it."

"Myca," she cried out. "Come here, child."

The little girl pranced happily into the room and then paused, almost like she sensed Darrell's presence in the room. She looked around but didn't see anything out of place. Myca walked up to stand beside Carolina.

"You listen to your maw-maw. She is gonna teach you things you will need to know."

"Will I be a witch woman like you?"

"Better than me, child. Study hard, practice. I have something for you." Carolina reached into her pocket and pulled out the carved dog. She put the dog in Myca's hand, covering it with her own just like her Gran had done so long ago.

Myca nodded, a smile on her lips.

"It's time for me to go now honey, your old Gran is tired. I wish I coulda seen 100 though. Only needed a little more time."

Darrell pointed up at the small clock on the wall. "Look at the time. It's after midnight. You made it, Chicken. Happy Birthday."

Carolina smiled. She'd made it: the dog had given her the extra time she needed. She lay back to rest her eyes, only for a minute, no more. The black dog padded close and nuzzled her hand.

Casablanca Z

Some cities don't fall. They rot from the inside out.

Chapter One

A City That Eats Its Own

"The lights are dying, and so is the city."

It's Lke an itch you can't scratch, this thing that gnaws at your innards until you want to scream. I can remember a time, not that long ago, when this city didn't sleep. Nightclubs closed just long enough in the wee hours of the morning to mop up the blood and booze, the whores that worked the bazaars barely got a moment's rest, and a person felt almost safe walking down the well-lit streets despite it all. Well, as safe as they could be, anyway. Casablanca is still a town of conflict, after all, with the French and the Germans vying for position. Now, I dunno. The city is dying, along with its people. And there is nothing in the world anyone can do about it; I sometimes doubt if anyone is even trying.

A streetlight flickers at the end of the street as I watch, the light flashes on and off a couple of times and then goes dead. Third one this week. Soon the whole town will be dark. That's when *they* will finally win.

I usec to love the city; the people pressed shoulder to shoulder jostling for space, the smells of food cooking in open-air markets, and bazaars with stacks of spices permeating everything, the pretty girls with dark eyes and knowing winks. Now?

Now I can barely wait to get out of here. That's not going to be easy, though.

I hear a scuffle on the street below my third-floor window, noises barely heard in the darkness. There used to be a streetlight there, too. Indistinct shapes shamble along in the gloom, their feet dragging on the pavement, their guttural voices moaning in the night.

The scuffle turns to a brawl and someone screams out. Gun shots. A common enough occurrence, but close enough to concern me. I turn my eye downward again but can't see anything. There is nothing to see but indistinct shadows playing across the sidewalk in the moonlight. Two more shots and then silence. Poor sap.

The sound of a motor cuts through the black night and pulls me away from what I can't see below me. This is what I have been waiting for, the reason I stand at this window each night. The motor whines, raising in pitch, like a mosquito in your bedroom, maddeningly taunting you in the night. I squint into the darkness over the buildings, toward the warehouse district. There it is.

Lights rise up out of the fog, three red beacons of hope, one flashing.

The plane lifts higher into the night, angling toward the water not far to the north. It swoops over the city, silver belly barely clearing the tops of the buildings. Anti-aircraft guns ring out a deep staccato. A line of tracer rounds follows the plane's progress, coming dangerously close to the tail section. And then the guns fall silent as the plane makes its way across the water.

The plane grows smaller as it flies away, taking a small part of my heart with it. One of these days I will be on that plane and can say goodbye to this city and its people. Not so much the live ones, but certainly the dead ones. The dead ones can all take a flying leap…

Someone bangs on my door and I glance over my shoulder.

The frosted glass shows the silhouette of three figures standing there, two giant men flanking a smaller one.

"It's open," I yell.

I see the shorter of the three twist his neck like he's working out a kink and then he pushes the door open. I recognize the man as soon as he walks in. Great. Just who I don't need in my life.

"You the private investigator?" The man's voice grates on my nerves. Ten seconds and already I don't like him. Maybe it's his reputation I have a problem with. I don't know the man personally. Perhaps I shouldn't judge. Then again…

"That's what it says on the door."

"You trying to be funny?"

"Not trying, per se, that's just how it works itself out sometimes. Call it a happy accident."

I study the three standing there, blocking the doorway. A lesser man would feel quite intimidated by their imposing figures. Good thing I'm no lesser man.

Eddie Manetti stands there, short and stocky. I always figured he would be taller somehow. I guess his reputation really does precede him. He's powerfully built and well-dressed, despite the fact he is covered in fresh gore, just like his two goons.

"Trouble finding the place?" I ask, glancing at the dark spots on his suit. "I'm kinda out of the way."

"Cut the chit-chat. I have a job for you."

OK. Now this is interesting. It wouldn't be the first time I'd worked for a local mob boss, but it would definitely be the first for someone as connected as Eddie Manetti supposedly was. What could someone like him want with someone like me, a broken-down PI with one foot in the grave already?

I walk across the room and sit one butt-cheek on the edge of the desk and pull a cigarette from a pack of Camels in my pocket.

I light it up and take a deep drag, enjoying the rush of nicotine to my system.

Eddie's eye twitches with impatience, waiting for me to continue.

"Who says I'm looking for work?"

Eddie pushes his chin up in the air and scratches away a bit of gore from his neck, wiping his fingers on his pants. He turns his steel-gray eyes on me, beady little orbs set too close in his face.

"Everyone is looking for work around here."

I glance out the window at the sound of a single gunshot ringing out in the night, followed by a woman's scream.

"These are dangerous streets. A man doesn't go out unless it is important." I pause for effect. "Or worth it."

Eddie stares at the ceiling, hands on hips. He sucks at a tooth, the edge of his lip curling up and tugging at a slight scar that runs across his chin.

"I'm sure a deal can be made that is…" Eddie pauses, thinking of the word he needs, "amicable."

Nice choice. My curiosity is piqued, at least. "So, what's the job?"

Eddie reaches inside his coat pocket and I freeze, ready to react. He pulls out a cigar and holds it up. "You mind?"

I shrug.

Eddie clips the end and jams it in his mouth. I watch the nipped end roll around on the floor, coming to a stop against the leg of a wooden chair. I wait while he lights it and puffs heavily on the stale cigar. I wrinkle my nose at the acrid stench.

"These are tough to come by these days," Eddie says, holding the slightly green cigar out. "You don't know what I have to go through just to get these."

"Lots of things are tough to come by these days, like food, and body bags."

"For some," Eddie shrugs.

"But not you?"

Eddie waves the cigar in the air like a wand. "I have my little secrets."

I begin to tire of the word-play. "This job?"

"I need you to find someone for me."

Unexpected.

"I'm still here, listening."

Eddie grinds his teeth together, his jaw muscles working. "I need you to find my fiancée. She's missing."

"Missing? Or just gone?"

Eddie locks eyes with me. "What's the difference?" Something doesn't feel right about this. He says his fiancée is missing, yet he doesn't seem that broken up about it. He asks me to find a woman, just as emotionless as if he asked me to help find his favorite tie clip.

"There is a big difference. Missing implies by nefarious means; gone could simply mean she left of her own volition."

Eddie stares at me blankly, mouth hung open slightly. I can see his tongue tapping his upper incisors.

"What word is tripping you up, Manetti? Nefarious? Or volition?"

Eddie grinds his teeth harder until I can actually hear the pearly whites gnashing together.

"You tryin' to be smart?" One of Eddie's goons slips a hand inside his coat. I can see him reaching for the obvious bulge there and I'm certain the gorilla's ham-sized fist is clenching a revolver.

I hold my hands up, placating him, then stand and walk around the desk, plopping down in my chair, grabbing a notepad. "So, what can you tell me about your, umm, fiancée was it?"

Eddie eyes me a moment longer, then nods and sits in the chair across from me, more relaxed. "Barbara Montgomery, everyone calls her Babs even though she hates it. She's a lounge singer."

"And family? Friends? I'm sure you have checked the places she likes to go?"

"No family, just another refugee stuck here like the rest of us."

"You have a picture?"

Eddie snaps his fingers and puts a hand up. Goon number one slips his hand in a pocket and pulls out a small photograph of Eddie and a pretty blonde woman. Eddie is smiling in the picture, his arm wrapped around her waist like she is a prize rather than a partner. That's how most men see their women I suppose, but it doesn't seem right.

Barbara looks to be an inch or so taller than the mobster, with shoulder-length hair cut in a classy style. Her eyes look like they might be blue, but the picture is slightly faded.

"What club did she sing at? Have you checked other clubs?"

"She sang five nights a week at Rick's Place, down by the market."

"Any other clubs?"

Eddie shrugs. "You know how many clubs are in Casablanca?"

I can't say as I do. I shake my head and study the picture. She could be pretty, but why does she look so pensive in the photo? "Are things OK between you and she?"

Eddie's eyes narrow even more. "What do you mean?"

"Everything peaches and cream? Fight a lot?"

"You know," Eddie begins. "A gentleman doesn't ask questions like that of another gentleman."

I nod. What's he hiding? "A gentleman also takes off his hat when he is inside." I see the red rise in his face, but there are things I need to know. "Is there someone else? On either side?"

"Mind your own beeswax. Look, do you want the job or not? I've got half a mind to just walk out of here and have the boys deal with you."

I know I should tell him to take a hike, to take his money and go find someone else to be his errand boy. The streets are dangerous, and I don't want to spend a lot of time on them. But the money could come in handy. An exit token costs money, a lot of money. And that is one thing I'm lacking. If I am to have any chance of getting out of this city, I'm going to need a token. They won't even look at you unless you have a token. Believe me, I've tried.

"I want the job." It galls me to say I want it to the man. I tell him my fee, sure he is going to try to talk me down. It's three times what I would normally ask for, but Eddie doesn't even flinch.

"Fine," Eddie says, standing and stubbing out his cigar in the cheap tin ashtray on my desk.

"Half up front," I tell him, pulling a receipt book from a battered drawer.

Eddie puts his knuckles on the desk and leans in close, eying me up. "Carlos, pay the man."

The crude business of money exchange happens and Eddie heads for the door. He stops and turns to me. "I will be back in a few days for a status update."

"I look forward to it."

I push my chair back and go back to the window, lean against the frame and peer out into the night, contemplating my next moves. I'm suddenly that much closer to getting away from the city. I turn my eyes in the direction the plane went, daydreaming about staring out the tiny windows, watching the lights of Casablanca slip away, replaced by white-capped waves as we fly off to Europe and freedom.

JC Rock

Chapter Two
Red Lipstick and Red Flags

"Nothing good ever follows a scream in Casablanca."

Two days of searching and nothing. No sign of the woman, not even a whisper of where she might be. It's like she's dropped off the face of the planet. I start to fear for the woman's safety. The streets aren't safe for man or beast, or missing lounge singers. I need to know one way or the other so I can pass that info along to Mr. Manetti.

I sip at a glass of bourbon in the Club Royale, listening to some redhead chop away at *Don't Sit Under the Apple Tree*. She isn't bad, but I don't think I will ever see her in a movie. Not with that voice. And not with those legs.

"Sorry," the man behind the bar says. His accent is as choppy as his mustache, and just as dark. "But this woman I have not seen. A singer, you say?"

I nod and shake the ice around in my glass. Over the strained sounds of the redhead, I hear a scream in the street outside, followed by several gunshots. The front door opens and another shot rings out in the night.

A skinny man plops a battered gray fedora on the bar and sits down beside me, wiping sweat from his brow with a stained handkerchief. His hand shakes from the effort.

"You OK?" I ask him.

The man smiles wide, and I swear I can count each of his teeth. He's nervous, trying too hard to appear calm.

"I will be. I had a slight run-in outside. I was fortunate the security was on hand. I thought this was a safe zone." He glances down at his jacket and fingers a hole in the sleeve. He brings away a bloody finger. "Oh dear."

I help the man slip his jacket off and right away everyone can see the bloody outline on his crisp white shirt.

He's been bit. The words echo in hushed whispers around the room.

Blood drains from the man's face. It looks like he is going to pass out right there. "That's me done for, then."

"You don't know that."

"I should have just stayed home. I was getting stir crazy."

"Why did you come out? You know the streets are dangerous." The bartender leans over, handing the man a glass of dark liquid.

"Same reason everyone does," he says, looking at me with his dark eyes. "For a bit of normalcy in a world turned upside down. A bit of drink, a pretty voice in their ears. That's why the markets are still open, why the carpet sellers still cry out their prices."

I nod, and suddenly the singer's voice isn't as bad as I thought it was at first. Perhaps that is what I am here for as well. It's clear Barbara isn't here, so why do I linger? It's not for the swill they call bourbon. I swirl my drink around again. Normalcy. But what is that? Is it normal to sit and drown your troubles in a bottle of bourbon and listen to a pretty girl sing a song while the dead roam around just outside the doors?

The *new* normal I suppose.

The bartender plops another drink down beside the man. "On the house."

"I guess I'm done for, if the bartender is giving away free

drinks." The bitten man looks at me. "How long do I have?"

I shrug at him. Who knows. I've heard stories of those going quickly, and others of those who lasted days, or even weeks before getting sick. Maybe it has something to do with one's constitution. As sickly as the man looks, I figure he doesn't have long at all. "Maybe you won't turn," I tell him. A little bit of hope never hurt anyone. "I've heard stories."

"Really?" the man looks at me, big brown eyes hopeful. I don't have the heart to tell him no. Why should I? "Sure, sure."

I turn back to my own glass of bourbon and tap the rim for the bartender. He tops me off. "Just leave the bottle. Me and my new friend here are gonna have a few drinks."

The bartender nods at me and I see him frown a little. I know what the man is thinking. He's thinking that this poor sap already looks sick, and he's going to die right here in the club.

"Don't worry," I tell him. "I will take care of everything."

I give him a knowing wink and the bartender nods as I drop a few bills on the table. I pour more into the man's glass.

"She's pretty," the man says, picking up the picture from the bar. "I feel like I have seen her someplace before but can't remember where. My mind is all befuddled."

"You have a name, friend?"

"Thomas."

"Well, Thomas. How long ago do you reckon it was since you seen her?"

Thomas shrugs. "A day, two. Three? I don't really know. I can't seem to think straight."

The man is turning faster than anyone I've seen before. I feel for him. And his family, if he has one.

"Come on Thomas, think."

"I'm trying," He yells at me, drawing the eyes of nearly everyone in the club. "Can't you see I'm trying?"

I hold my hand out, calming him. The rage has already set in, that's easy to see. I need to get him out of the place before things go from bad to worse.

"Sure, kid. It's not important. Come on, let's get you to a medic station."

Since the outbreak, small clinics have popped up around the city to take care of the injured. Cuts and scrapes and gunshot wounds. Too many of those. The living were having just as big an impact on things as the dead were. And more importantly, an aid station was specially equipped to deal with those turning. A single gunshot to the brain, destroying it, was all it took to quell the rage that burned in the walking dead.

I grab Thomas by the arm and help him stand. The other patrons closely watch what is going on with a wary eye. Can't say as I blame them. The night clubs have become a bright spot in an otherwise dark life. If the dead invade this place, then there is nothing left.

The redheaded singer belts out a high note, drawing eyes back to her, and allowing me to shuffle Thomas along to the door without any hassle. Three dark figures block the door, just out of the pool of light spilling out of the club.

"Mr. Nelson," The voice says with a thick German accent. Casablanca is a French colony; for the moment, anyway. But since the war I've noticed a much-enlarged German presence. I suspect it has something to do with the American base further south.

"That's me," I say, narrowing my eyes. Not sure I like Germans knowing my name. "What can I do for you?"

The kraut licks his lips. "A word is all I require. It won't take but a moment of your time."

"Time is something I ain't got a lot of right at the moment. I need to get my friend here to one of the clinics."

The German looks Thomas over, notices the bloody spot on his arm and his eyes narrow. "He is bit? Please, allow my men here to assist him while we have a quick word."

"And who am I having that word with?"

"I'm am Oberstleutnant Wilhelm Manks." The man stands a bit straighter, pushing himself just that little bit higher than his fellows.

I study the three of them. Each one is cut from the same cloth; a hulking, muscular cloth full of attitude. The guns at their hips and the rifles slung over their backs steal any argument from me. I pass Thomas over to their care, and the German who spoke steps in closer.

"Shall we go back inside? I hear the singer here does a passable version of *Edelwiess*."

I watch the other two drag Thomas along the sidewalk, stepping around the concrete barriers set up as roadblocks for the dead. They turn a corner into an alley.

"Hey, where are they taking him?"

The German grabs my arms tightly and ushers me back toward the door. "To get the help he requires, of course."

Before we go into the club, I hear a single gunshot ring out in the night, echoing off the buildings. Poor Thomas; perhaps it was best this way.

The German leads me to a table in the corner of the room and sits, ordering a bottle of cognac from a passing girl.

"That's expensive stuff, not like the normal bathtub gin most places have around here."

The German nods. "Yes, smuggled in from the east. We of course allow it. Comforts of home are a necessity."

I feel my ire raising. "You allow it? This is a French colony."

"For now, but so was Paris, and they let us walk right in and stay. Such a picturesque city, not like this place." He raised his nose in disgust, wiping away a bead of sweat from his brow as he took off his hat.

Best if I let the subject drop. "So, that word you wanted?"

He set his gray eyes on me, narrowing them to tiny points in the shadows of the corner. "You have been making inquiries, Mr. Nelson. About a certain missing person. Perhaps you would like to share your findings with us?"

Why does this man care about a missing lounge singer? I'm not about to give him anything. Not that I know anything to start with. About all I had learned so far was that she was—perhaps— alive a day or two ago.

"I'm not sure what you are talking about." I shrug. "Please don't play me for the fool, Mr. Nelson."

"It's Frank. *Mr. Nelson* was my father." Cliché I know. Still, it makes me smile. Not much does these days.

"Humorous," the German says, though it is clear by his tone he doesn't seem to think so. His loss. "Let me tell you what I know, Mr. ... ah, Frank. I know that local *businessman* Eddie Manetti has contacted you about his missing fiancée. And since that time, you have visited several clubs and made inquiries about the woman."

"And if I was, what is it to you?"

"I too, have an interest in finding this woman. Perhaps we could share what we know."

I feel my face heat up, suddenly feeling like I'm being played. I don't like that feeling. Just what is going on here? "Seems you know as much as I, perhaps even more?"

The German works his jaw like he wants to speak, then snaps his mouth shut and watches the redhead dance clunkily around the stage, with her green dress swinging out in a circle around her as she spins.

"As I said," he continues. "I have an interest."

The German lights a cigarette from a silver case, the flame causes shadows to dance across his face.

I've had about all the conversation with the man I can stand. There are still a few places I want to hit before the night is up, and travel in the city can be problematic to say the least. Keeping to the safe zones to get where you are going can be a challenge.

"I think your interest and mine don't intersect. Goodnight." I stand to leave and he grabs my wrist tightly. So tightly I can feel my hand go instantly numb.

He turns his gray eyes to mine. "Goodnight, Mr. Nelson. I'm sure our paths will cross again."

He holds me there another moment longer, then releases me. I nod and turn, pushing past the two other Germans who had returned. Glad I'm able to keep my anger in check.

The little run-in with Wilhelm made two things very clear to me. One: There are more people looking for Miss Montgomery than I know about. And two: Why would the Germans want her? I have no idea. But now I also start to wonder about Manetti's real reason for wanting his fiancée back.

A light breeze blows off the ocean, carrying the scent of salt and sand. There was a time when I enjoyed the scent, but now it is just one more reminder of how cut off Casablanca is from the rest of the world. Except for the few smuggler caravans who make the trek across the desert, and the daily air drops of needed supplies from the British military, there is little going in or out of the city.

The weekly charter plane that operates under the cover of night is the one ray of sunshine in an otherwise dark time, for those that have the money anyway.

I start down the street that will take me to my apartment when

I notice a small group of the dead shambling toward me. Five of them walk along, grouped closely together. That is a few more than I want to deal with alone. The revolver hangs heavy under my coat, but I'm not going to risk it. Not tonight. I don't need the noise bringing any more to me. Something bigger is going on here and I have this burning desire to figure out just what it is.

I cut across an alley, with a different location set in my mind now. It's time for me to pay an old pal a visit. My pace quickens when I hear a scream echoing up the street to me. The numbers of the dead seem to increase daily, which can only mean one thing: the numbers of the living have decreased by the same number—or more. All the more reason to get out of this city while I still can.

I turn down a narrow street with no name and can instantly feel the eyes on me. In the moonlight I see dark figures peering out over the tops of the buildings and flashes of light off of gunmetal. If there is one truly safe spot in the city, this is it. It's also the most dangerous. The black market isn't a place for the casual person. I slip through an archway and knock three times on the metal door, then wait a moment and knock three more.

A small peephole opens at eye level and I see a pair of familiar spectacles peer out at me. I see the brow furrow through the tiny slot. I move so the light from the slot can hit my face and I see the eyes go wide and the slot slams shut.

A clinking of dead-bolts and the door swings open. The smell of spices and alcohol and smoke assail my nostrils. When everything is mixed together it's a near sickening mélange of odors.

"Frank," the voice says. "What are you doing out here at this time of night?"

"I was in the neighborhood. ThoughtI would stop by for a chat." "Sure, sure." He slides the door shut and bolts it locked, then throws a piece of iron across it to block the door from swinging open.

Monty is a weaselly little man, barely more than five-foot six. Skinny and pale. He doesn't seem like much and most would assume he was a nobody, a petty functionary in a large crime syndicate, running the black market for those above him. They would be wrong. Monty has built up the whole thing himself. He's the one responsible for the hired guns on the roofs, the cacophony of smells from the warehouse, and the grunts of men and women in tiny rooms set apart from the rest of the place. He's also the one who contracts the plane that takes those lucky enough away from here.

"Coffee?" Monty asks. "Just got some from the last plane. Not much, so it is going into my personal stock."

"Sure, Monty. Sounds good."

He leads me to an area, just past stacks of spices in metal tins, that's set up like a small cafe where the smell of coffee is strongest, thankfully overpowering the other smells. At least in this one area. We sit at a small table and Monty waves his hand in the air at a pretty little blonde.

"How's business?"

I slip my hat off and set it on the table beside a pretty little floral centerpiece as the girl sets two cups down.

"A bit slow," I tell him. "But you know how it is. The dead roam the streets. Not many people need my services these days."

"So, what brings you here? Looking for something specific?" Monty sips at the coffee cup in his hand and purses his lips. "Not the best, but certainly better than nothing."

I look down at the table and the small cup in front of me. "Why so small?"

"It's the Turkish way. Very strong coffee. Not the way you Americans drink it, all watered down. I never understood that."

I sip the hot beverage and try to keep the sour look from my face. It's way too bitter for me, but I must admit that the little rush of caffeine into my system is a welcome friend. It has been too long since I've had coffee, even bad coffee.

"I was wondering…" I start, not really sure how to broach the subject. "The travel tokens. Has the price come down any? I'm having trouble raising the money."

Monty purses his lips and shakes his head slowly. "Sadly no. If anything, the price has doubled. I nearly lost the plane the other night."

I nod to him. I had seen the tracer rounds following behind the aircraft. Every time I had seen it, the rounds were drawing closer and closer. That just makes it even more important that I get out of the city before the flights stop all together. I should have gotten out early, before the ports closed, before the blockades on the roads out. Hindsight is a funny thing.

Now the only options are to buy a travel token on the single plane that runs or hook up with one of the caravans that head across the desert. That has its own dangers. There is a war on, after all. The few caravans that make it into the city tell tales of giant herds of the dead roaming the wastes, and the German army is causing trouble as well.

It's just not right. I suppose I can understand why they closed the ports. Africa is lost, but from all the reports I've heard, the rest of the world seems to be fine.

I choke down another sip of the bitter coffee. It's all too much to bear sometimes.

"Are you sure there is nothing you can do about the price?" Monty shrugs his shoulders and the white shirt he wears billows out. "Sorry, my friend. You are already getting more than a fair deal. Anyone else would pay half again as much as what I am offering you." He smiles and a gold tooth winks at me from between thin lips.

I slam the cup down on the table, breaking it. I jump up and grab the collar of the stupid shirt he wears and jerk him from the chair. "You have to do better. Dammit, can't you realize I need to get away from this place?"

I hear the cocking of guns and screams coming from the small stalls in the makeshift bazaar. I look up and see men standing around me, rifles all pointed at me.

Monty hangs limply in my grasp and puts his arms out. "Stop, don't shoot him. He is a friend. Right, Frank?"

My eyes dart around to each one of the guys holding rifles on me. Why had I done that? Recently my fits of anger were getting worse, set off by the smallest of things. I drop Monty back into the chair and he straightens his shirt.

"Sure, a misunderstanding is all." I smile at the men and sit back down, smoothing my nerves down as best I can. "I... I'm sorry, Monty. I don't know what came over me."

It's a tough thing to apologize to someone, especially for me. My mouth often gets me in trouble. Rarely does my temper. Seems the city has a hold on me. It's almost like being cooped up in your own room for too long. Stir crazy they call it. I hadn't considered leaving Casablanca before, but now that I can't, the desire is even greater, and I suppose it grates on me. Gnaws at me.

"Sure, sure." Monty picks up the bits of broken cup from the table and slips them onto a tray the waitress brings him. The men with rifles fade back into the background. "You know, Frank, you really are getting the best price I can offer, because you are a friend. Those don't come often in my business. I will overlook your little indiscretion, just this once."

I nod and wipe the sweat from my brow. Why is it so blasted

hot in here? No one else seems to feel it.

"Listen, I picked up a job looking for a missing woman. Was wondering if you have heard anything."

I fill him in on the few details I have, leaving nothing out. He nods and sips at his coffee. I even tell him about my run-in with the German officer and his men.

I finish my tale and Monty sits there looking at me for a few minutes like he's sifting through tidbits of info in his brain. "I may have heard something about this woman," he starts. "Manetti's fiancée, you say?"

I nod and pull a cigarette from the pack. Last one. Looks like a good time to quit. "A real piece of work, that one."

"Oh yes, I'm familiar with Manetti. We have crossed paths once or twice. He tried to muscle his way into my business. My boys made sure he got the message he wasn't wanted. He came here a few times after that, buying expensive gifts for his girl. Real pretty, blonde haired, blue eyed. He wore her on his arm like a prize. More property than anything. Like she was just there for him to show her off."

"I'm starting to get that idea myself."

"So, she's the one you're looking for? What did she do?"

"Gone missing is all I know. Starting to wonder if it isn't more of a case of she's hiding, rather than missing."

It isn't the first time the thought has crossed my mind, and something tells me it won't be the last.

"So, what do you know about her?" I ask Monty.

"Huh?"

"You said you may have heard something about the woman?"

"Oh, sure, sure." Monty scratches the stubble on his chin. "She's a singer, right? I heard there was a new club open. In an abandoned building. Not part of any ring."

I nod at his words. Most of the clubs, the questionable ones anyway, are part of a nearby crime boss's organization. They operate independently, but use the gangsters for protection, offering a cut of the proceeds for their services.

"Some building? Is that the best you got?"

Monty shrugs. "On the other side of the bazaar. That's all I know."

I stand and grab my hat, slipping it in place and tilting the brim low to shield the lights from my eyes. They have been really sensitive lately. "Thanks Monty, I owe you one."

Monty nods. "I will add it to the list."

As I step out into the night again, I realize I am dripping sweat. Funny. The heat has never bothered me before. Probably the coffee. I never understood drinking a hot beverage when it is so hot outside. That's the French way, though.

I make my way across to my own place; a shabby place in a whole row of shabby places. I can see a couple dead milling around at the end of the road and they turn almost as one and head toward me. I was as quiet as I could be, how had they even heard me?

I fumble the keys in my hand and manage to slip the door open and myself inside before the dead make it even halfway down the street. Thank goodness the things are slow. Not sure how long the city would last if they had any kind of speed at all to them.

Being dead seems to have taken the steam out of them. They shamble along, sometimes even crawling along, their rancid clothes dragging behind. One thing is for sure. Only a head shot takes care of them. Destroy the brain and you give a final underline on their death certificate.

I make my way up the steps and finally hear the dead pushing against the door behind me. The door will hold, and the glass has wire running through it. It's held up so far, anyway. I slip through my office and back to the little flat I've called home for five years now.

The tiny space is little more than a simple cot pushed into the corner, a table and chairs near the door, and a cook-top that rarely sees action. I make my way to the tiny bathroom and flick on the bare bulb above the mirror. Sweat beads on my brow so I run some cold water in the sink and splash my face to cool off some. My insides feel like I am on fire and a red mist covers my eyes.

I grip the edge of the sink tightly and squeeze my eyes shut to keep the voices from whispering in my brain. I worry about the things the voices are telling me.

I open the medicine chest with shaking hands and pull out a bottle of aspirin, dumping out half the bottle into the palm of my hand, spilling several down the drain of the sink. It had cost me nearly ten times as much as it would have just weeks before, but the headaches were getting worse and I needed some relief. I chew a handful of pills dry, not even washing them down with water in hopes it would hit my system that much faster, then examine myself in the mirror.

My blue eyes are bloodshot and don't even look like mine. Sleep has been a distant memory to me for days on end. I can't even remember the last time I slept through the night. Every time I close my eyes the voices invade my brain, only growing louder the longer I ignore them. It's only through sheer exhaustion that I fall asleep anymore. I snap the light off and head back into my little room, spying a bottle of bourbon sitting on the table. That seems to be the only thing that helps me sleep nowadays.

Chapter Three
Deals and Dead Men

"Hope is a plane ticket and half a bottle of gin."

I glance at the watch laying on the small table beside me. Three-fifteen. Judging by the light outside, it's not in the morning. Meaning I slept through the entire day. When I sit up, my head swims around and I have to put a hand on the table to steady myself.

When I'm finally able to stumble my way to the bathroom, I lean over and puke in the toilet, trying not to notice the small amount of blood I see there. My head pounds, but it is nothing compared to the fire in my belly.

By the time I wash up and dress, I feel almost human again. Funny how that works. I glance at the contents of my cabinets, wondering if something to eat wouldn't be a good idea. I don't really think so, not at the moment, so I head out the door after checking my revolver and the folding knife in my pocket.

I spend a few hours checking the clubs and back-alley bars that Monty suggested, but there really isn't anything to them. Most are just watered-down gin joints and a few fringe establishments that I would rather not have to visit again. They all have one thing in common: pale, haunted faces that look warily at me in the dim lights.

My legs ache from all the walking, but gas is at a premium and I don't want to have to pay for a cab anyway. I try to stay in the safe zones as much as I can, but most of the places I visit are off the beaten path.

I hear a scream behind me and turn just in time to catch a young woman running down the sidewalk toward me. She has that look in her eyes; the one that says she knows her time has come but is unwilling to let it come for her quite yet. She is going to fight the inevitable tooth and nail.

The woman runs down an alley. I try to stop her, but she slips from my grasp.

"Hey, lady!" I yell. "Stop! Come on, that way is blocked."

She runs down to the end of the alley and frantically tries all the doors and windows, banging like a mad woman and screaming to be let in.

I rush down the alley to grab her. She tries to pull away from me, but I hold her arm tightly and drag her back out. Except it's blocked.

Four of the dead shamble into the opening of the alley. Here in the confined space the smell of them is overpowering. I try to push my way past, but they have the entire alley blocked.

I let go of the woman and shove her backward behind me , slip the knife from my pocket, and open it. I hadn't been looking for a fight today, but it seems one has popped up looking for me. My stomach roils at the smell and the thought of having to put them down, and it's still not settled too well from when I woke up. I still haven't eaten anything, despite the fact I'm beyond famished.

I push the woman backward, deeper into the alley, past a pile of trash against the wall of one of the buildings. I need a narrow space, make it so they can only come at me one at a time.

The whole thing has a familiar feel to it. Just a week ago I had been in a similar situation, working to fight my way out of a tight spot. I swore then I wouldn't do anything as stupid again, and here

I was. Stupid accomplished.

The woman won't stop screaming. If she isn't quiet, she is going to attract more of them, and I'm not sure I will be able to handle those I currently have.

"Shut up," I hiss at her. "You're making things worse."

The woman collapses into the corner of the alley, her ear-shattering screams thankfully turning to quiet sobs. I feel bad for her, but there is little I can do for her at the moment. I have my own troubles. If I survive this then I will get the chance to help her out. I try not to remind myself that she is the reason I'm in this mess in the first place as I reach for the first of the dead.

His fingernails scrape against my skin. I keep him at arm's length and try to get a good jab into his ear canal with the point of my blade. A sickening crunch echoes in the alley as the knife pushes into the dead man's brain. He drops instantly, almost jerking the knife from my hand.

Before I even have time to recover my stance, the next dead pushes through the narrow spot between wall and trash, tripping over the first and tumbling forward into me. I stab out with the knife but miss, scraping against his shoulder blade. I wince at the feel of steel grating against bone.

The third dead stumbles in behind him, her pale gray hands reaching out for me. This is taking too long. I drop the knife and pull my revolver out from underneath my jacket. I'm not the best shot in the world, but at this close range even I should be able to hit the target.

I aim down the barrel at the dead woman's head. When I pull the trigger, her head explodes in a shower of pinkish mist. The top of her head blows away and flops down, hanging on only by a narrow flap of skin. The dead man on the ground grabs my ankle, almost pulling me down to the ground.

I can't get a good bead on him as he tries to sink his teeth into my ankle. No sir, buddy. Not this time. I raise my other foot and stomp down on his head.

It takes a few stomps, but I finally feel the head give way under my foot with a crunching sound. The huddled woman mews behind me and I can hear her being sick as I turn to face the final dead man trying to pick his way through his chums on the ground as they start their forever sleep. I don't want to fire my weapon again, but the knife is on the ground someplace.

I draw a bead on the dead man and fire a slug right through his forehead. Like with the woman, the top of his head explodes outward, spraying brains and blood and bone against the wall. I stand there leaning against the wall, breathing heavily as the dead man drops to the ground.

I feel hands on me and I turn quickly, raising the gun barrel up, remembering in time that it is only the woman behind me.

"Is that all of them?" The woman peers down the alley, waiting expectantly for the sound of movement. When nothing comes, she looks at me. "Thank you."

"Are you OK?"

"I ... I think so. I got separated from my husband. Can you help me find him?"

Any other day I might have said yes. But my stomach roils and my head swims from the effort of even keeping a fresh thought for more than a second. "There is a safe zone just two blocks away. Just turn right out of the alley and you will walk right to it."

"But you have to help me," she pleads. "What will I do without my John?"

"Look lady, I did help you. But that is all the time I have for you today. Go on, scram!"

I don't mean to yell at her, that's just how it comes out.

The woman looks at me, bottom lip trembling slightly. "Ass." She straightens herself up and walks down and out of the alley, turning left.

"Miss?" I yell out to her.

She turns and glares at me, hands on hips, waiting impatiently. "Right," I say to her, pointing the way to the safe zone.

She spins on her heels and huffs off in the direction of the safe zone. She's better off that way. Find someone that can help her. I certainly can't. Most days I can't seem to help myself.

I bend down to hunt for my knife in the gloom of the alley and feel a shooting pain in my arm and fluid oozing.

When I pull my jacket off and slide my sleeve up, it's clear that the wound on my arm is still open. It's been ten days and still it won't heal.

I pull the gauze off, wincing when it pulls at my skin, and examine the nasty-looking bite mark there. The edges are getting black and a sickly black bruise is creeping up my arm, with black tendrils following the veins of my arm. Time is running out for me. I know this. I've known it for days. The fever, the anger issues. I've seen it all before in dozens of others. I had hoped … No, I *still* hope.

Ten days is longer than I've known anyone to last. I still have time, but I need to get out of here. I'm sure the doctors in a real city, a city that still lives, will be able to cure whatever this is. It pisses me off knowing that I'm so close to getting out of here, and yet so far away.

I fix the gauze back in place and pull my sleeve back down. No one else needs to know about my condition. After what happened to the young man the other night … It seems the Germans have found their solution to the plague, or whatever this is.

I find my knife and wipe the gore off on one of the dead. I'm sure he won't mind. With a bit of care, I'm able to slip my jacket on without hurting my arm too much. I'm getting to old for this kind of work.

The next address on my list is just a few blocks away and I head off in that direction, hoping for a bit of luck.

Chapter Four

Her Voice, My Cure

"She sang the madness right out of my blood."

The big, bald bouncer at the door eyes me up and down, noticing the blood on my jacket. I shrug. What is there to say? I'm sure he has seen worse. He nods and lets me through the door with a gentle reminder that there is a minimum drink order. Not a problem. After the day I've had, a few drinks will sit pretty well, I think. Somewhere along the line my stomach has settled itself. Perhaps I will even have a little food if it looks clean enough inside. Some of the joints I'd been in so far, I wouldn't trust any food served there.

The joint is actually pretty decent inside. Not up to the standards of the main street clubs, but still. For the times we are living in, I'd say the proprietor has done a good job of keeping things looking nice.

I bypass the tables spaced evenly around the dance floor in favor of a cushioned seat at the bar. That's where I am going to end up anyway, might as well start out there. I order a gin and tonic after the bartender tells me they are out of bourbon. I light a cigarette and settle back to try and stop the shakes that have returned. The red tinge is back over my vision.

The band starts to play the first few notes of *Bewitched, Bothered, and Bewildered.* And then *she* walks out to the center of the stage to raucous applause. There isn't any denying that she's the one I'm looking for. Her eyes scan the room and I swear my heart skips a beat when her eyes meet mine. She starts to sing and it's like the heavens have opened up, letting the angels out.

From the very first notes that spring from her, the red tinge over my eyes fades and a calmness comes over me. And not just me; the whole room seems entranced.

I'm wild again. Beguiled again. A simpering, whimpering child again. Bewitched, bothered and bewildered am I.

The bartender plops the glass in front of me on the bar, but I barely notice. I sit there watching the woman sway back and forth as she sings.

Her eyes sweep across the room and lock with mine again and for a few seconds I find myself jealous of Eddie Manetti.

The headache that had been pounding its way through my brain for several hours fades away, not even a distant memory of its being there. Such is the power of Miss Montgomery's voice.

Before I know it, the song is over and it takes a long moment for me to regain myself. I feel a small amount of emptiness when she stops. At least, until she starts walking across the room toward me, applause following in her wake. She almost floats across the floor in her dark sequined gown, until she is standing beside me. With her this close to me, even the wound on my arm seems a memory

"Buy me a drink?" Even her speaking voice seems a balm to my brain. From someplace in the back of my mind I remember what I'm here to do and I manage to shake off some of the effects of the woman.

"Sure," I tell her. "Gin? They are out of bourbon."

"You a bourbon man?" Barbara sits on the stool next to me and spins it around, feet out and swaying.

I nod, watching her smile like a child as she spins, her long, brassy blond hair flying out behind her.

Barbara puts a hand on the bar to stop the spin and looks at the bartender. "Two glasses of what you have under the bar," she says, keeping her voice low. She turns to me. "Can't stand gin. But Billy's got some nice stuff tucked away, in case of emergency."

"Is this an emergency?" I try to sound coy, unsure what coy is supposed to sound like.

She laughs, and it echoes off the walls. For a second, I feel the same euphoria wash over me. Her eyes twinkle in the lights of the club, like two crystal blue pools of water.

"No, not an emergency." Her voice takes on a slight tinge of sadness. She puts her hand out. "I'm Barbara Montgomery. And you are?"

"Enchanted," I say, trying to sound clever as I reach for her hand. "Also, Frank Nelson."

"Well, hello, Enchanted Frank Nelson." Her hand is warm as I hold it. I feel this connection to her I can't explain. I think she feels it, too. She fights to pull her eyes off mine and grabs the glass sitting on the bar and downs it in one gulp, closing her eyes as the dark liquid eases its way down her slender neck.

I smile dumbly, apparently the only way I know how, and once again try to come up with something clever to say. Nothing comes to me. Typical.

Musicians start to play a few notes, preparing for the next song.

"Stay here," she tells me. "I have to go sing again, but I want to talk with you more. OK?"

"Sure, sure. I will be right here, counting the minutes." Smooth. Real smooth.

Barbara stands and turns, her fingertips brush against my hand and I feel shivers race up my spine.

She swishes her way across the dance floor as the band starts playing *Putting on the Ritz*.

I swirl the bourbon around in my glass, realizing I hadn't even tried it yet.

"You bit?"

The bartender's words catch me completely off guard. I know how the average person feels about the infected. Maybe not to the same extremes the Germans took with poor Thomas the other night, but still the end result is about the same. I feel the blood drain from my face.

The bartender looks at me. "It's easy to see you have felt her power."

The bartender grabs my glass and pours another one for me. I start to wonder at the cost of that glass. I try and wave it away. "On the house, my friend. Miss Montgomery hasn't sat and talked with anyone like that the whole time I've known her. She just hides herself away in her little room. If she wants to share with you, so do I."

I study the thin man behind the bar. On a quick glance he could be one of a dozen bartenders across this city. On closer inspection I see the sickness around his eyes, the redness. The dry, cracked lips. The hands shaking, just barely noticeable.

Barbara starts to sing, and I see his face calm, along with my own. The feeling of well-being washes over me again. I turn my stool to watch her and notice the crowd. Knowing the look now, I can easily count those that are infected just by the looks on their faces as she sings.

Billy leans his elbows on the bar. "You can see it too, now."

I nod. It's an easy thing to see and I chide myself for not catching on sooner. I'm supposed to be the observant one. It's kinda in the job description, after all.

Barbara sings across the stage. From time to time her eyes flash over and catch mine, each time pulling a shiver up my spine that ends as a smile on my lips.

"How long has she been here?" I ask Billy as he hums along to the tune.

"A week? Two? Time is difficult to keep track of these days. So much death. The dead roaming the streets, the Germans close behind. Gangs of thugs killing each other. Everyone wants a piece of this city."

"In the end, it's the dead who will win."

"You are right, my friend." Billy grabs my empty glass and refills it.

The music fades low as Barbara's high note echoes off the walls of the tiny club and all is silent. The euphoria slowly dims in my mind, but the red rage stays hidden just under the surface.

Barbara walks across the dance floor toward me, ignoring the praise of the people she passes. Her eyes are on mine, a slight smile on her lips.

"Please," I tell Billy before Barbara gets there. "Don't let on I'm infected."

"It's not my place, friend."

Barbara sits beside me on the stool once again. Her perfume washes over me and I smile.

We talk through the night, about nothing, really. Our dreams we know will never happen, the war, how I think she should be in movies. She smiles at that and my world lights up. It is easy for me to believe I could have feelings for the woman with little effort at all.

The club closes and I reluctantly make my way back to my tiny space, an aching in my head, but an indescribable feeling in my heart.

Chapter Five

Bitten Truths

"You don't need a bullet to die here—but it helps."

The match burns down almost to my fingers and I wait until the last moment to light my cigarette, blowing the match out. There is something about the smell of the burnt sulfur that is soothing.

Night presses against the window, threatening to burst its way in and carry me off into the night. My fingers shake from the fever racing through me. I eye the bottle of gin sitting on the desk, my last, and half-empty. One or two more good nights and that is all she wrote.

The power is out across the whole city as far as I can tell. It lasted much longer than I figured it would. It's candles and cold beans with sandwiches from now on. However long that is. The bite on my arm burns like fire while the rest of me shivers. I wonder idly if it would be better to just cut it off and be done with it. I push the thought aside, not wanting to go down that path again. One thought leads to another, and then another. Pretty soon I'm sitting on the toilet, pants around my ankles and the barrel of my pistol between my teeth.

A heavy banging on the door steals the thought away before it's fully formed. Pity, it was starting to sound good.

"Yeah?" I pull my pants up and head toward the front office.

My voice cracks when I call out. "It's open."

I have a sneaking suspicion who it is. I've been waiting for him to call around.

The door swings open and Eddie pushes his way in, followed by the familiar bulk of the two thugs who seem joined at the hip.

Eddie stands there and glares at me, waiting. I'm really not in the mood to have to deal with him today. I know what he wants. I'm just not sure I want to give it to him.

"What can I do for you?" I sit at my desk and unscrew the cap on the gin. My head is pounding. All I want to do is sleep. But even that is a folly. Most nights I just stare at the cracks in the ceiling.

"Any progress on finding Barbara?"

I study his pockmarked face. There doesn't seem to be any redeeming qualities to him. He stands there, face like a stone, waiting. No emotion on his face at all. This man doesn't care about Barbara. He probably doesn't care about anyone but himself, and that seems iffy.

"I've had a few leads, but nothing concrete so far." I lie to him. He's not the first client I have ever lied to. Probably going to be the last, though. "I just need a little more time to hunt down some people that might know a thing or two."

I feel small sitting there in the chair with the bulk of the three men hanging over the desk. I grab a glass and pour some gin into it, then stand and walk around to sit on the edge of the desk. Cigarette smoke burns my eyes, making me squint.

"Drink?"

Eddie shakes his head. "I've given you plenty of time, and money, and you don't have anything to show for it."

"Not exactly nothing," I tell him. I'm losing my patience quickly. "I ran into an interesting fellow. A German officer, in fact." Eddie's eyes narrow and he squints at me. His jaw muscles work overtime under the pockmarked skin.

"You know the fellow then," I say. "Seems he is looking for your *fiancée* as well. Why is that?"

"You ask too many questions," Eddie says.

"Questions are part and parcel of my trade."

Eddie's eye twitches. He's getting aggravated, I can see. He pushes a stubby finger against the middle of my chest. "Just find her."

Red covers my eyes and I grab Eddie's finger, giving it a twist until I hear it snap. Eddie yelps in pain and jumps back. Goon number one steps forward and slugs me across the jaw. Stars explode in my vision, all tinged with red. I act without even thinking.

I grab the man's arm and twist him around and press the palm of his hand against his back. He squeals, and I pull his arm up higher and higher. I don't understand the strength I seem to have. Perhaps it's just born of rage, or something in the fever that is slowly killing me.

The man stands on tip-toes, trying to ease the pressure on his arm socket, but I don't relent. I raise his hand up higher still and the shoulder joint finally gives way with an audible pop. The man screams as I let his wrist go.

There is a flurry of movement at the corner of my vision. I spin around, hands up in a fighting stance, ready to take on anything that might come my way. Except a gun. The cold barrel of Eddie's pistol steals any fight I might have had in me. There are times when a man stops and takes stock of his life decisions. This is one of those moments. I can't say my whole life flashes before my eyes, but several parts of it certainly stroll by for a bit of introspection. Staring down the dark barrel makes a man think, you know? With a little imagination I can almost see the head of the bullet, ready to leap from the chamber and bury itself deep in my brain. Maybe that's the best thing for me.

"Gimme one good reason to not put a bullet in you right now." Eddie twitches and his hand shakes a bit. No doubt he has found himself in this situation before, but I can't imagine him ever having to pull the trigger himself. I'm sure he delegates the job to someone with a bit less scruples and morals than even he has.

I put my hands out to the side and shake my head. Thoughts whirl through me and I try to catch a few as they pass. All to no avail. Why shouldn't he kill me? My mind is blank. I know I should be able to come up with a dozen reasons or more why he shouldn't.

"I'm not ready to die," I manage to croak out. A feeble excuse at best, but it seems to disarm him a bit and his hand wavers.

Sweat beads on my face and runs down under the collar of my shirt uncomfortably.

Eddie squints at me then leans forward, examining me like some strange bug under a glass. "You sick? You've been bit, haven't you?"

I don't know how he can tell. I could simply have a fever. As near as I know there are no other outward signs. I nod at him.

"I was bit on the arm." I slide my jacket and shirt up to show him the blackening wound. The teeth marks are easily visible, and the black streamers running away from the wound seem to pulse with a life of their own. My heart thuds in my chest.

Eddie lowers the weapon in his hand, but doesn't put it away. "Can you believe this?" Eddie turns to the other goon standing there cradling his twin's arm, trying to keep the pressure off the destroyed joint. He turns back to me.

"I seen a man give in to the fever. A friend. The spasms at the end liked to have snapped his back in two. It was the nicest thing I could do, putting a bullet in his brain. That's why I'm not going to waste one on you."

I almost want him to. I've seen what the end is like and I have no desire to reach that point. When the time comes, I will put a bullet in my own head.

"You dying like that," Eddie shrugs. "Best punishment I can think of. You OK with that, William?"

Eddie turns to the man with the busted shoulder and the big man nods feebly. The look on Manetti's face doesn't give him much choice but to agree. "Sure, boss."

"On second thought …" Eddie pops open the cylinder on his revolver and pulls out a single bullet. Candlelight gleams off the brass surface. He stands it up on end on the desk. "Keep that. For the end. Put it to good use. Let it be the one that ends your miserable life. Forget about Barbara, I will find her on my own. Consider yourself fired."

Eddie ushers his men out of the room and it's another minute before I realize I still have my hands up. I grab the bullet and walk around the desk, plopping myself back in the chair. The bottle of gin calls to me and I slip the bullet in my pocket. Maybe I will take Eddie up on his offer to use that bullet.

Chapter Six
The Bullet You Keep

"Some favors come with a receipt. Some
with a funeral."

I slip through the safe-zone barrier. Three days ago it had been manned by five people, today only two gun-shy looking young men keep a wary eye on the darkened streets. I've seen it all over the city. Another day or two and this safe zone will be down as well. It's hard to worry about the safety of others when you are worried about your own survival.

"You gentlemen OK?" I pause to have a word and see if I could bum a smoke from one of them. Up close they appear even younger; boys barely out of school. Where is the army? The Germans are running all over the town, and the French are holed up in small conclaves. No sign of the Americans we had heard about to the south. I know there is a war on, but a concerted effort of manpower could wipe this city clean of the dead.

"Yessir, right as rain," the young black man says in a thick Moroccan accent. "You got business here?"

I tell them I'm going to the club and give the man a dollar for a single cigarette. Most I've paid for one by far. I slip it behind my ear and head for the club, leaving the scared young men guarding my back.

The doorman recognizes me and nods as he opens the door. Nice work if you can get it. I notice the bulge under his jacket and realize he is more for security than greeting people.

The cool interior of the building welcomes me. Ceiling fans still run, slightly stirring up the air to make it the least bit bearable. They must have a gennie running someplace. I close my eyes and listen, but I can't hear the hum of it.

The club is crowded, but I notice a small booth in a darkened corner of the room and make my way there. Barbara is there on stage, her voice instantly calming me. I catch her eye and give her a little jerk of the head.

Billy brings me a glass of bourbon without my asking. "On the house," he says. I don't know how he stays in business, but I have never turned down a free drink and I ain't about to start now.

Barbara finishes the final notes of *Don't Sit under the Apple Tree* and takes a slight bow during the applause, none louder than my own. The band slips into an easy jazz tune and Barbara makes her way over to the booth, smiling happily.

"I'm so glad you came back," she says. "Oh my, what happened to your jaw? That looks like it stings."

I smile despite myself, my jaw hurting when the skin pulls back. "You should see the other guy."

"You lead a dangerous life, Mr. Nelson."

"I suppose." I think about Eddie again and the rage bubbles up inside me. The man had really gotten under my skin. That is something that doesn't normally happen. The reason for that sits next to me, her perfume wafting over me, subtle and sweet. "You don't have to worry, though. I'm not on that job anymore. Things fell through."

"Oh, Frank, I'm sorry."

I shrug. It's so easy talking to her. I wish I had met her months ago, before all of this. Would it have been the same?

"So, what now?" she continues.

"Same as always. I need to find a way out of this place, away from the dead. It just might take a bit longer than anticipated. What about you? If you could get away, would you?"

"I'd like to think I would. But it's not that easy, at least for me."

"Why?"

"I …" She wants to tell me something, she's just having trouble. I don't want to push her.

"You can tell me, I won't tell anyone."

Barbara twirls the drink Billy brought her. She looks out at the few people holding each other close out on the dance floor. Her eyes have this faraway look, like she is remembering fond memories.

"I'm hiding here. This club."

"Who are you hiding from?" I'm happy she trusts me enough to tell me the truth.

"My ex-boyfriend. He was a real jerk and just couldn't take it when I left him."

"Some guys just can't take a hint."

"You don't know the half of it. Eddie was … not a nice man. You know he hit me once."

I can feel the anger well up inside me again, the red tinge covering my eyes. If I had my druthers I'd go back in time and put a bullet between his beady little eyes. I might still do that. Not the time part, but the rest of it. I feel the bullet in my pocket with my fingers. Somehow it's become a comforting weight, a talisman against the insanity that rules the city.

"A fellow like that isn't worthy of a woman like you."

Barbara blushes at my words, and it just increases the feelings that I have for her. I've only known the woman a short time but feel like it has been a lifetime. I want to spend my days just listening to her talk. And sing. Imagine that, a hard-boiled guy like myself cracking up over a dame and going soft.

"I'm nothing special," Barbara says sadly. "I guess I just have bad taste in the men I chose."

"Perhaps you just haven't found the right one yet." I lean in close to her hoping that she would get the message I was trying to send her.

Barbara bats her long eyelashes and leans closer and I see her lips part. Nothing ventured, nothing gained. I kiss her, briefly, and the red tinge fades. The rage that had been in my brain just a moment ago is nothing but a lingering memory.

She pulls away from me and fans her face with her hand. "Oh my, that was unexpected. I … I barely know you. And yet, it feels like we have always known each other. Do you understand?"

I nod at her. "Run away with me."

"Where?"

"It doesn't matter. As long as we are together, it doesn't matter. If this whole thing has taught me anything at all, it's that you need to make the most of life, while you still can."

I want to tell her about the bite. I can feel it itching as a reminder, almost like it is forcing its own will against mine. I push the feeling aside. No. Barbara can never know. We will get out of this and I will get some proper medical care. Someone will figure out what this is and they will cure it. As long as I have Barbara, as long as she can sing, then I know I won't turn.

"How will we do that Frank? We can't leave, they won't let anyone leave."

I glance around the club to see who might be listening. Everyone seems to be in their own little world, dealing with their own little issues.

"Do you have any money?"

Her brow furrows as she looks at me. "A little, why?"

"There is a way out," I tell her in a low voice. "A plane that comes in and out every few days under the cover of darkness. We can be on the plane, for a price."

I can see the hope in her eyes. "I don't have much. The clubs don't pay what they used to, and everything is so expensive. But whatever I have is yours, if you can get us on that plane. We could run, just like you say. Any place in the world."

Barbara tells me how much she has stashed away. It isn't enough, not by a long shot. I try to keep the disappointment out of my voice.

"I have some stashed away myself, and a few people still owe me a favor or two. If they are still alive. We might not be able to make the next plane, but maybe the one after."

I just need to find a way.

The band changes up the tune and Barbara stands. "I need to get back to it. Will you be here when I get back?"

"I might head out and call on one of those people who owe me a favor."

Barbara leans in and kisses my cheek quickly and rushes off to the stage, breaking into song. I sit back and let her voice carry me away, a calm falling over me like a fog. She truly has the voice of an angel.

"She is something, is she not?" Billy places another glass on the table in front of me and sits down.

"That she is," I reply. "There truly isn't another like her."

"Does she know?"

"Does she know what?" I narrow my eyes at the swarthy individual.

"That Manetti hired you to find her."

"What makes you think that?" Damn bartenders always know too much. I guess that is what makes them the go-to guys for private eyes like myself.

Billy shrugs. "I notice things, I hear things. The Germans are looking for her, too."

"I think you know too much for your own good. No, she is safe. I won't be giving her up."

"I'm just looking out for her safety." Billy looks at me with his dark eyes. "I don't know what I would do if anything happened to her."

"You in love with her?" A feel a jealous pang in my stomach.

Billy laughs. "Oh no, nothing like that. Maybe ... Maybe as one loves a kid sister."

"Nothing wrong with that." I tell him. I had a kid sister myself.

"And you. Do you love her?"

"I barely know her."

"Still. I can see the look in your eyes." Billy scrunches his chin up. "And hers, too. If you can really get her out of here, please do it."

I glare at the man for eavesdropping. "I'm going to do my best. Can you tell her I had some business to take care of?"

Billy nods. "Sure, sure. Have a good night, Mr. Nelson."

I nod at him and slip my hat on, throwing a smile at Barbara as I walk across the floor. Her voice follows me out the door and into the night. As soon as the door clicks shut behind me, the red tinge starts to creep back into my vision. It's a near-constant thing now. And it's troubling.

Chapter Seven
Men in the Mists

You never know who's more dangerous:
the dead or the disappointed.

I tip my hat to the young men manning the safe-zone barrier and head off down the darkened street. Only moonlight covers these streets now, blanketing the corners in deep shadows. The silhouette of two men on the other side of the street catches my eye. They don't walk like the dead and I'm instantly alert. These days the living are just as much a danger as the dead. I recognize the bulk of them, the cut of their suits and the way they hold themselves. Manetti's goons. They are way too close to the club for my comfort. I've got to head them off at the pass. No way am I giving them Barbara now.

I slip across the street and call out to them. "You fellas lost?"

One of them slaps his friend across the chest with the back of his hand. "Look, William. It's our old pal. How are you, Frankie baby?"

"That's Mr. Nelson to you."

William glares at me and I notice the sling holding his arm tight against his side.

"Hey, listen chum, about the wing. Sorry." I mentally check the weight hanging against my chest inside the jacket, thankful I remembered to pack my pistol. I don't think this is going to end well. I'm not sure for who quite yet, though. "No need to hold a grudge."

"You busted my shoulder, asshole." William's voice is deep and booming, the polar opposite of earlier when I had him squealing like a little girl as I popped his shoulder out of its joint. "I think that is reason enough to hold a grudge."

"Eddie's looking for you," the other pipes up. "Seems he has had second thoughts about letting you continue to breathe."

I'm instantly on guard, pretty sure I can take both of them down before they can react. But there is one thing I need to know.

"So, what brings you gentlemen down here? This ain't part of Manetti's block."

He shrugs. "We are expanding all the time. Soon we will own this city."

"I'm sure the dead will have something to say about that. And the Germans."

Red creeps across my vision and a tiny little voice in my head starts to scream at me to kill them. To rip them open. Beads of sweat runs between my eyes, stinging in the heat of the night.

"But if you must know, Boss got word about where Barbara might be."

My heart pounds in my chest. There is no way I can let them find her. I need to put them off the trail, somehow.

"A club? Down here? Only one I know of *does* have a new singer. A pretty little redhead."

It's not much, but enough to make William furrow his brow and look at the other. "She ain't got red hair."

"Shut up, William." He looks at me and smiles. "You wouldn't be trying to trick us, would you?"

"You got me," I say, holding my hands up slightly at my sides. "Just having a laugh."

The guy reaches under his jacket and pulls his pistol from its holster, pointing it at me. This is starting to tick me off. I've had too many guns pointed my direction recently. My heart thumps harder and harder and the little voice in my head grows more insistent. These men need to die to keep her safe. I'm not a violent man, but I do what's needed to protect myself, and my own.

But the tide has turned. Thirty seconds ago I could have taken them both out easily, and I should have. Now … now things are a bit more complicated.

William fumbles with his left hand, trying to pull his pistol out. I remember he is right-handed, so his holster is on the wrong side.

I push off with my foot and barrel into William, who is still trying to retrieve his gun. He goes falling backward, his arm flailing in the air trying to catch his balance. If he had use of both arms he just might have made it. As it is, he crashes down onto the dirty sidewalk, falling on his bad shoulder and screaming out loud. He's out of the fight, at least for the time being, but I still have a man behind me, with a pistol drawn and two good arms.

I kick my foot out and swing around, trying to catch the gun in his hand, or at least catch him off guard. No such luck. I traveled too far when I pushed William down and my leg sweeps through empty air dramatically, but ineffectively.

The report of the pistol echoes down the alley behind me and I hear trash cans clatter somewhere down in the darkness. The heat of the bullet grazes my face as it passes. A bit too close for comfort.

I reach to pull out my pistol, but the missed kick has thrown me off balance and I tumble to the ground. That's probably what saves my life as a second bullet whistles by. I can hear the air splitting by my ears.

A groan comes from the alley and in the dim light I see two shambling figures. Things are about to get *really* interesting.

My hand slips under my jacket and finally closes around the butt of my pistol and I yank it out of the holster. Did I remember to check the rounds? No time now.

I bring to pistol's barrel to bear on the man as he steadies his own. He yelps in pain when I pull the trigger. He drops his pistol and grabs for his thigh.

Even in the darkness I can see the patch of wetness spreading on his pants. The man is bleeding out quickly. He drops to the ground with a groan.

The shambling noise grows louder and I turn back down the alley and see the dead creeping ever closer.

William rolls around on the ground, still in obvious pain.

The rage roils inside me, unchecked. I want to drop down to the ground and rip the two men to shreds for even thinking of threatening Barbara like that. In my past, I haven't been a very violent person, but events of the last few weeks have brought it out of me like some primal urge that was always there, hidden just below the surface.

In the past I would have helped William up and gotten him away from the dead. Now I bend at the waist and catch his eye. "You brought this on yourself."

I cross the street and slip into a darkened doorway to watch as a few more dead shamble down the street, drawn to the sounds of gunshots. Noise always brings them. William screams as the first dead falls on him and rips at his throat with gnashing teeth.

There is a perverse pleasure in watching the dead devour the men and I catch myself licking my lips. Some weird little voice in my head urges me to give in and join them. I push the voice aside. I'm not quite ready to give up just yet. I know the time is coming.

I *need* to get out of this place.

Chapter Eight
Blood Debts and Bad Luck

Even dying men make promises.

The first contact I check with is a nonstarter. He owes me money, sure. Not a lot, but some. It might be enough to make a difference. The steps of the old French Colonial lead me up to the second-floor landing. I knock on the door, waiting. I almost turn to leave when I hear a weak voice say *come in*. I twist the knob, on guard as always, and peer in through the crack. In the darkened room beyond I can see a gaunt figure sitting at a small dinette near a window; bright sunlight streams in through the colorful curtains. Dwayne smiles weakly when he sees me. The dark bags under his eyes, and the feverish brow, tell me there is no help to be had here.

A pistol sits on the table and I eye it warily as I sit down across the table from him.

"I don't have the strength to pull the trigger," he says. "Guess I waited too long, huh?"

"Ya, I reckon so."

"You don't think you could do it for me, could you?"

It's not the first time I've heard such a request, and I doubt it will be my last.

"Sorry, chum. I just can't. I hope you understand."

I can't give him a reason why; I'm not sure I know it myself. That's just a line I'm not willing to cross yet.

We share a drink, and I share a sandwich from my coat pocket, giving him the lion's share. It isn't much, but it might sustain him another day, but I know that soon he will be part of the great horde of dead.

I nod at him. Not much I can say to that. *He* seems to have accepted his fate, no reason I shouldn't.

I need to get moving. I've already spent too much time chewing the fat with the man. I stand, joints creaking in the silence of the room. When I pick the gun up I see the hopeful look on his face, that falls only a little when I cock the hammer back and set it back on the table. That should make it a little easier. Dwayne nods at me, his shallow eyes watery in the dim light. I leave him with some sympathetic words I almost believe and step out of the tiny apartment into the darkened landing. Before I can get my foot on the first step heading down, the sound of a pistol shot rings out in the room beyond. I guess he found the strength after all. Maybe the sandwich helped.

The sun beats down on my face and it is glorious, even though it burns my eyes and makes my skin itch. The sun still shines as the city around me dies. Perhaps future generations will be able to once again enjoy the beauty that is Casablanca, but for now it is a place of death and decay.

I make my way across town, trying my best to keep to known safe zones, but so many of them have fallen over the past few days. I manage a mile or so and find myself trapped between two small groups of the dead. I wasn't paying attention. It's stuff like this that makes a man dead real quick.

I slip down an alley and quickly duck behind a pile of trash, hoping they pass me by. The rusted ladder of a fire escape hangs above me, frustratingly out of reach. I nestle down in the trash and listen, straining my ears for even the slightest sound, the smallest hint that they followed me down the alley.

I hear the dead pass by the alley, and then a few stragglers shuffling behind the main group. In the heat of the day the smell of them is overpowering, especially when mixed with the acrid odor of the piled trash. I wait for what seems an eternity and then risk a glance around the trash. I don't see anything.

When I move from behind the trash, I trip on a coiled piece of rope and fall into the pile. Tin cans go skittering from the pile, noisily clanging as they roll along the pavement.

A couple of dead slip into the alley.

I reach for my gun, but push the thought aside. With so many dead so close, I can't take the risk of drawing them to me. I fish around in my pocket for my knife and have a moment of panic until my hand closes around the heavy metal object.

The blade clicks into place when I open it and I stand, trying to find a good place to defend myself. This is the third time in as many days that I have gotten myself into trouble. Pretty soon the odds are going to catch up with me. Hopefully today ain't that day.

The woman reaches out for me and I can see the skin peeling away from her fingernails, crusted in blood and gore. White eyes criss-crossed with veins of black stare back at me. I don't even know how they can see, but somehow they do.

I push out at her and my hand pushes through her ribcage and hangs there. When I yank my hand back, bits of skin come back with it and I gag at the slimy feel of it. I throw my other hand forward, stabbing out with the knife and poking it into her eye. Black ooze dribbles down her cheek as I push the knife even deeper, probing for her brain. Once the blade has destroyed enough of it, she drops like a sack of potatoes.

There is still one more to take care of. He was a well-dressed man, once. Remains of a crisp white shirt hang loosely from him underneath a sharp-cut jacket. He reaches out for me with a hand that has several fingers missing, broken away somehow to slightly bloody stumps. I bat the hand away.

He pushes on toward me and I can't get a good swing at his head with the knife. All I can manage is to keep him at bay as I shuffle backward. Too far. I find myself with my back against the wall, arm extended and hand against his chest. The remains of his fingers scratch at me, pulling away the skin at my neck.

My hand creeps up his chest and clamps around his neck and I squeeze it tightly, forcing him down to the ground so I can stand over him and drive my knife into his skull. The strength of the dead man is incredible, but I soon get my leverage and I'm able to push him down once his legs finally give way to the added weight of my own body. He drops heavily to the ground and I jump on top as he grabs at me with his dead hands. I put my knees in the middle of his chest to hold him down and manage to grab one flailing arm and drive the knife in through his ear canal, silencing the man forever.

The fight leaves me winded more than I would like to admit and I just roll off the dead man and lay there on my back, trying desperately to catch my breath. It's a good thing there were only the two of them because it takes me several minutes to be able to sit up and dust myself off. I can feel blood running down my neck and inspect the wounds gingerly with my fingers. If I hadn't been bitten before, this would have definitely done the trick.

The wounds don't feel bad, small cuts more than anything. I straighten my jacket, intent on making my way home to clean up before I head out later to see Barbara. The thought of her brings a smile to my face.

Some glittering piece of metal laying on the ground beside the dead man catches my eye. The contents of his pocket have spilled out onto the trash-strewn asphalt and a glittering bit of gold stands out among the detritus. I stoop to pick it up and know instantly what it is. My heart thumps heavily in my chest again, almost to bursting. I didn't think I would get to see one, to hold one in my hand. But here it is, and I am elated.

It won't do the man any good, not any more. But the travel to-ken I hold in my hand means a way out. Luck has finally turned around for me. The small bit of metal in my hand makes up for all the bad that has gone on.

I gather the other items and stuff them in my pocket and turn to search the woman. Perhaps ... I dare not hope.

Nothing. I didn't really expect anything, but ...

I make my way back home and clean up, a smile on my face. I can't wait to show Barbara. It's still light when I am done, so I lay back on my small cot and close my eyes, just for a bit, and drift off to sleep. For just a few hours the red tinge and the rage racing across my brain is forgotten. I have a way out.

Chapter Nine
Run Like Hell

One last chase, one last lie, one last night.

I wake, with the token still clutched firmly in my hand, and sit up.

I turn the token over in my hand, flipping it end over end between my fingers. It's a crude piece of metal, hastily stamped with a series of symbols. And a date. Why hadn't I noticed that before? I rub at the dried blood on the token, wiping it away to clearly read the date stamped into it. Today. My heart thumps in my chest. I have what I need.

It's too early an hour to go across town to the club where Barbara sings. Still, I can't wait to see her. Two safe zones that had been operating just hours ago were now overrun. The city is losing even faster now, gasping its last breath. If I have to make a guess, I would say it has days at most. Shame.

There isn't a guard at the door as I pass into the dim interior. It takes a moment for my eyes to adjust to the gloom. No ceiling fans whir to stir up the stagnant air, no electric lights, either. Smoky oil lamps cast small pools of yellow in a few spots around the room.

No band plays on the stage, and there's no Barbara singing. A moment of panic sets in before I see her blonde hair at the bar, shining like a beacon in a vast, dark ocean. The bartender notices me and nods, drawing Barbara's attention.

Barbara turns, and when she sees me her easy smile splits even wider and she nods me over to join her.

"Frank," she says when I sit down beside her. "I wasn't expecting you so soon. I'm glad to see you, though. We will have some time before I need to sing. The club doesn't officially open for another fifteen minutes."

"No time, baby. We need to get out of here."

"And go where? Frank, I can't just pick up and leave."

"I got us a way out. A way out of Casablanca, and away from the dead. This city has reached its end. It's time we get out of here."

"Do you mean it?"

"Sure baby, I got our ticket to ride."

I don't have the heart to tell her I only have the one token, and that I intend it for her. She won't come with me otherwise. I grab her hand and help her off the stool. "We don't have much time."

A voice from behind makes my blood run cold. Eddie Manetti. Just like a bad penny, he keeps turning up. "You two ain't going nowhere. Hi, doll. Miss me?"

I notice the pistol in his hand, aimed right at my gut.

"Eddie?" Barbara turns pale and I feel her hand tighten on mine. "What are you doing here?"

"You think I could just forget about you? You and me, we got things to take care of."

"I told you, I don't want to marry you. I'm getting out of here, tonight." Barbara's voice shook.

I explore my options. They seem few and far between, and all of them involve going through Eddie. Far too many steps between here and the door, and three men with guns in between. "With him?" Eddie waggles the gun at me. Then bursts out laughing.

"What's so funny?"

"He didn't tell you, did he?"

"Tell me what?" Barbara looks at me, a question in her eyes. "He's working for me. I hired him to find you."

Barbara puts two and two together and comes up with betrayal. I can see the hurt in her eyes, but she doesn't betray me to Eddie. "He told me. He also told me he was fired. None of that matters, anyway."

Eddie's hand dips, ever so slightly. It's the only chance I'm going to get. I grab the heavy bottle of bourbon from the bar and smash it against the side of Eddie's head. He drops like a ton of bricks to the floor.

There is a gunshot behind me. The bartender has slipped a rifle out from under the bar and shot one of Eddie's men. "Run!" he yells, waving the shotgun around to the other goon.

I don't wait for an invitation. I pull Barbara along behind me and barrel my shoulder into the other man, pushing him to the floor just as he fires off a shot aimed at the bartender. I hear a slight groan behind me, but don't hang around to see what has happened.

We rush out the door and I look around, spying Eddie's car parked on the corner. In the sky above me, I hear the heavy whine of a plane descending. We don't have much time. The location marked on the token is fifteen minutes away, easy. I don't reckon the plane will hang around long.

I pull the passenger door open and shove Barbara inside, then run around and get in myself. I push the clutch in to engage the starter and we are off a moment later. I hear gunshots echoing behind me and something pings off the side mirror, shattering the glass. Is that seven years of bad luck for me, or the guy who shot it? I slide the car around a corner and to safety, plotting my course across town.

We drive along in silence for a few minutes and then Barbara speaks.

"Is it true? Were you hired to find me?"

No sense lying. "I was. And I was also fired, just like I told you."

"Did you tell him about me? Where I was?"

"I didn't. He knew I was lying about not knowing where you were. He even put a gun on me to make me talk. That's why he fired me."

"So, I was just a job to you?"

How can I explain to her what she is to me? She doesn't know I'm sick. Or at least she hasn't given me any indication she knows. "When I first met you, sure, but that ended quickly. From the moment I walked into that club and saw you, heard you singing, I knew I couldn't give you up."

I turn to look at her. The moonlight plays a symphony across her face, sad and sweet, a tune played far too often. I can see tears on her cheeks. She nods in the darkness.

"Now what?" she asks.

"Now we get out of this place. Find someplace to go where the dead don't roam the streets."

"What if they are everywhere?"

I hadn't considered that. What if Casablanca was just the start? Was it even?

"We can't think like that. We need to have hope that there is safety out there. The plane comes each week, like clockwork. If the whole world was dead, I don't think they would bother."

Barbara nods. "OK."

We make our way across town to the tiny airstrip that has been cut in a field. Halfway down the runway stands a battered and beaten hanger with no doors. It's easy to see it has been hastily built out of tin and salvaged wood. Dim light spills out onto the dewy grass and I can see the tail of the plane sticking out of the opening. I steer the car down the access road, narrowly avoiding a crater in the middle of the road, a reminder that we are still at war.

I pull the car into the small parking lot and notice the other cars in the lot, along with a German officer's vehicle, the redand-black Nazi flags flapping slightly in the breeze. When we get out, I can hear shouting coming from inside the hangar.

I peer around the corner of the building and it takes my eyes a minute to adjust to the light. The silver plane dominates the space, oil smoke and steam coming from its twin rotary engines. Across the tail fin I see the blue, white, and red of the French flag. People look nervously through the tiny porthole windows at the scene playing itself out in a pool of yellow light at the bottom of the plane's steps.

The German I had run into before, Wilhelm, holds a Luger in his hand, pointed at a man I can only assume is the pilot. He has that look to him, anyway. Aviator jacket, cocky attitude, and baggy pants with far too many pockets. It looks like they have finally caught up with the smugglers. But where are the other men who traveled with Wilhelm?

I study the deeper shadows of the hangar. The place is empty except for a few barrels and boxes that have been unloaded from the plane, ready for pickup. Why is Wilhelm here by himself? I'm not going to argue with my good luck.

I draw my own revolver and check the bullet count, then add a few more from my pocket to replace the spent rounds. I walk into the hangar, gun out, and walk up to within thirty feet of Wilhelm before he realizes I'm even there. The pilot's glance in my direction triggers Wilhelm. He spins and points the gun at me. We stand there, each with guns drawn and not saying anything.

His jaw drops when he sees the girl several paces behind me. I told her to stay hidden, but just like a dame she didn't listen.

"Herr Nelson, I see you have brought me a present. And just my size, as well."

"I'm no one's prize," Barbara says, walking up to stand beside me.

"I'm sure many would disagree." Wilhelm looks at Barbara.

"Please, Miss Montgomery, won't you come over here and join me. And you, Mr. Nelson. Please do put your weapon on the ground and slide it over here to me."

I lock eyes with the man, trying to take his measure. He turns the gun slightly and points it at Barbara. "I'll not ask again."

I'm sure he wouldn't shoot her. Not after all the effort that everyone put out to find her, but I can't be absolutely sure. I hold my hands out to the side and bend over slowly, watching for an opening. It's the pilot that gives me that chance.

The pilot swings his fist and catches Wilhelm on the back of his head. It probably doesn't do much to him at all, but it is all the chance I need. I drop down to the ground and roll to the side, bringing my gun up to draw a bead on him and fire. All before Wilhelm even has the chance to realize what happened. The bullet tears through his stomach and he drops to the ground like a sack of rotten German potatoes.

The pilot rushes forward and grabs the pistol Wilhelm drops and stuffs it in his waistband.

"Is it too late to catch the plane?" I hold up the token so it catches the light.

The pilot takes it from me as Barbara slips an arm around my waist, giving me a gentle squeeze. He gives the token a quick glance and nods. "You know … you know this is only good for one person?"

I nod. "Give us a minute, will you?"

The pilot nods and walks over to sit on the stairs leading up into the plane.

"Frank? You said we were getting out of here. *We*."

"Sorry, baby. This is the end of the line for me. I think I've known all along I wasn't getting out of here."

"I don't understand."

"I'm sick. Bitten by one of *them*."

I see tears well up in her baby blues. It breaks my heart to see her cry like that. "Why didn't you tell me?"

"I was hopeful, I suppose. In the end that is all we can have. Hope. With your singing keeping the rage away, I was hopeful I could get out of here and find a real doctor to cure whatever this is. I see that's not going to happen now."

"It's funny," she says, wiping a tear away. "With the world crumbling around us, we pick now to fall in love."

I know she feels the same way I do. "Sounds like a bad movie, Barbara."

Barbara shakes her head. "No, it sounds like a wonderful movie. My Bergman to your Bogart."

"I bet if they made a movie together it would be terrific," I tell her.

"Frank," she continues, kissing my cheek. "I can't leave you like this."

The sound of car doors and gunfire stop any reply I might have had. I shove Barbara toward the plane. "Go on, get out of here. Live."

Barbara hesitates. I can see the indecision on her face. Then she turns and runs to the plane. The pilot helps her up the steps and then climbs in himself.

"I will hold them off best I can." I yell to the pilot. He doesn't even hear me. He is already closing the door and a few seconds later I can hear the engines coughing to life.

I spin and dodge behind a stand of barrels just as Eddie and one of his men turns the corner in to the hangar as the plane slowly starts to move. I fire off a shot, making the stubby gangster dash for cover behind some boxes.

The plane spins around in the small space of the hangar and heads for the door, moving terribly slow.

Eddie dashes toward the plane, pistol out and firing at the windows by the pilot. I fire my own pistol, catching him in the thigh and making him spin across the rough gravel. I rush forward, firing as I go.

The plane finally eases free of the hangar and turns down the runway. Eddie fires at me again and I feel a deep pain in my gut and fall to the ground, firing as I fall. I hit him right between the eyes, a round dark spot forming as he falls forward.

I hit the ground and roll over. There is still a threat, but the thug has turned tail and run. A dead comrade and a dead crime boss probably makes him double think his decision to enter a firefight with me. That's probably a good thing. I'm not sure I have any more bullets in my pistol.

I manage to stand, but the pain in my gut makes me double over and puke on the ground. I wipe my mouth with the back of my hand and make my way out of the hangar, just as the plane is turning at the far end of the makeshift runway. Red tinges my vision as I make my way to Eddie's car and lean against the door, propping myself up.

I button my coat up, hiding the blood-stained shirt underneath, and fix a smile in place. I don't want her last image of me to be one of a dying man.

The plane pauses at the end of the runway and then I hear its engines rev up and lights start to bounce down the field toward me.

The tail section raises up off the ground as the plane levels itself for takeoff. As it passes by me, wheels barely skimming the ground, I catch a glimpse of Barbara in one of the porthole windows, smiling sadly at me. I manage a wave, ignoring the pain in my belly, as she passes by. The plane lifts off into the air and banks right, heading for the open water to the north.

I see tracer bullets follow its path through the night sky, but they never even come close to the plane. Another group of refugees have gotten away from this god-forsaken place. Godspeed to them.

I slide down the door of the car and sit on the running board, wiping away the sweat on my brow. I'm not really sure which is going to claim me first, the fever or the gunshot. I know I should just put a bullet in my brain to save myself the knowledge I will be adding my own corpse to the great horde of dead, but I can't seem to raise my hand again. The pistol feels so very heavy in my hand. I feel the weight of Eddie's bullet in my pocket, but can't seem to raise my hand to retrieve it.

All I want to do is sleep. I close my eyes, for just a second, and it feels so good. Sleep it is.

Wings Over Staria

*If the sky was meant to be unreachable, it shouldn't
have opened its arms so wide.*

Chapter One
Cinders and Cogs

*Every machine needs a spark. I just didn't
think it would be me.*

Mary Stewart walked into the cramped room and pushed the door closed behind her, locked it, and started unbuttoning the heavy bustle dress she wore, eager to be free of the weighty, constraining fabric. Her mother would have made her stay in it all afternoon if she hadn't managed to sneak away while everyone else watched the juggling act. She slipped free of the dress and pulled on some comfortable and familiar suede pants with a knit pullover, then examined herself in the full-length mirror mounted on the back of the door.

Mary didn't like the way her mother had done her hair so she swept it back into a loose ponytail, something much more fitting of a twelve-year-old girl on holiday. She started to take off the small locket around her neck, but decided to keep it, tucking it, instead, under her shirt. She liked to keep her baby sister Beatrice close. Mary still didn't know why Beatrice was left behind. Beatrice was ten after all; there were lots of children on the ship the same age, some were even younger. Her mother was getting tired of Mary's complaints about the subject.

Mary plopped down on a stool at the end of the bed and slid on a pair of leather boots. She was still breaking them in and they hurt her feet, but they were so pretty with their silver bands and bits of tortoise shell embellishing the sides. She stood and stomped her heels down into the stiff boots, pleased with the tinkling sound the small silver chains wrapped around the heels made.

The ship listed to the side and Mary had to catch herself against the dresser. This had been a constant thing, and not the least bit enjoyable to her. She'd wondered since everyone boarded why people even took cruises in the first place. There was little room to play, and no one seemed to want to do so anyway. All the older people did was sit around, and eat and drink, and talk about things that were happening back home. They could have done all of that at home, and Mary would have had the massive backyard for her and Beatrice to play in.

Mary waited for the ship to right itself, then opened the door. A porter glared at her when she stepped into the hall like she was some bug under inspection. Children seemed to be an unwelcome thing on the ship. She smiled and waited until he passed around the corner, then rushed for the stairs.

Once on the upper deck, Mary stepped into the sunshine, letting it splash across her face. She had the whole deck to herself. With a bit of imagination, she could pretend the whole ship was empty of everyone but her. She wondered why everyone preferred the closed-in spaces below when it was such a wonderful day on deck.

Mary pushed her sleeves up, wondering what game to play. Whatever it was, it was going to be by herself. She'd made several attempts to play with the other children on the cruise, but they all seemed just as bored - and just as boring - as the adults. They preferred eating too much and playing the machine games in the penny arcade. Mary gave them a try too, but they didn't hold her attention for too long at all.

Mary hopped over several deck chairs, chanting, "Boring. Boring. Boring."

She couldn't wait to get home. America had been fun to visit, but she was ready to be home again with her sister. Her father said they were only a couple of a hundred miles away now. It wouldn't come fast enough for Mary.

The sun was strong on the deck, so Mary reached into a pocket and pulled a pair of sunglasses out, marveling at the way the thin blue glass caught the sun. She slipped them on, smiling at the slight blue tint everything had. She bounded toward the front of the ship, intending to stand as far forward as she could, far away from the thumping of the engines down below and the billowing black smoke from the dual smokestacks. It had to be horridly hot and smoky down below where the engines were. Maybe she could get permission to pay a visit. She didn't think her mother would allow that. To Mary it sounded like a perfect chance to get a little dirty. She and Beatrice regularly got into trouble back home, often coming in covered head to toe in thick red mud from behind the stables. Her mother was definitely anti-dirt.

Mary ran down the aisle, jumping the deck chairs like the hurdles she'd seen when the whole family went to the athletic games in London. She darted around the swimming pool, wondering why no one was there. Then she remembered the magic show in the auditorium. Mary didn't think that would be very fun either, no more so than the jugglers that everyone marveled at. A meal and a show, that's all anyone seemed interested in. Everyone else seemed excited by the magic show. There was an escape artist from America performing some trick or other.

Mary jumped over a few more deck chairs.

"Boring Boring. Boring," She muttered again.

Mary grabbed a broom from the corner of the storage bay and brandished it like a sword, beating back pirates that only she could see. Until someone coughed behind her.

"Miss? I'd ask you not to break my broom. I have cleaning up to do before the show is over." The woman smiled at her.

Mary handed the broom back sheepishly, then watched the old woman disappear behind a door that led down into the ship.

The ship leaned again, and Mary had to grab onto a railing. The seas were growing rough. It looked like a storm was coming. She could see dark skies gathering on the horizon. Storms came up so quick on the ocean; if she was going to see the front of the ship before it rained, she'd better hurry.

Mary jumped another pair of deck chairs, barely nicking one of them and it clattered over. She glanced around to see if anyone had noticed as she righted the chair. She stepped to a more open area and rushed to the front, a bit disappointed. Ropes and other mooring items filled the bow so she couldn't get all the way forward. Not a problem.

Mary climbed over the thick rope, catching her foot briefly in its coils. She climbed over stuff until she got to the front railing and peered over the edge at the bow as it cut through the waves. Mary frowned. She had expected a figurehead to be on the bow, like the ones she had seen on the bows of pirate ships from her picture books, but there was nothing but faded white paint and a bit of heavy chain clanging against a bare metal spot on the ship.

Mary stayed in the bow, watching the world go by until the rain began to sting her face. She thought it funny how one moment it can be sunny, and the next a squall. She squinted into the wind, then glared at the storm. Now she was going to have to go back below decks with the rest of the boring people. Maybe she could find some fresh fruit. Her favorite was pineapple because she thought it was exotic.

Mary turned to head back inside and the ship leaned once again to one side. She grabbed at the railing, hanging on. She felt a vibration travel through the deck. A great rumble echoed from below decks and the whole ship seemed to shudder and lean over even further.

Fire shot from the smoke stacks amidships, and the whole ship rocked again, seeming to groan in pain. Warning klaxons sounded, but only for a few seconds before fading away weakly. Mary wasn't sure what had happened, but knew it couldn't be good at all. She managed to climb over the ropes and other stuff, heading to find her parents. The ship leaned heavily over starboard, so far in fact that the lifeboats attached on that side scraped the water. A wave came and pulled a few of the small craft away from their lashings.

For a few minutes, the ship righted itself and Mary managed to find her footing again. She headed to the stairwell that led down to the auditorium. She had to find her parents and her older sister, Alicia.

Another explosion shook the ship, making it fold in the middle, the bow and stern raised up from the water. The ship buckled, and Mary lost her grip on the railing, sliding toward the edge. She squealed as she slid closer to the edge, her fingers scrabbling at the wood decking. She was so close to the edge her feet dangled over the side.

From somewhere over the noise of the ship dying, Mary could hear screaming, and realized it was the people below-decks.

The back of the ship burned and water splashed over the edge, soaking her. Mary struggled to pull herself away from the edge. Yet another explosion rocked the ship, sending her splashing into the water.

Mary knew how to swim, but with the heavy waves she could barely manage to keep her head above water. Bits of the ship filled the water around her and she had to dodge several sharp looking pieces of wood. She tired too quickly, and knew she needed to find something to help keep herself afloat.

Mary struggled against the waves, trying to get away from the ship as it burned. Her arms grew weak. If Mary didn't find something soon, then she wasn't going to be able to keep herself above the water.

Something bumped her in the back of her head. Mary screamed, gulping in a great mouthful of water. She nearly slipped under the surface of the water, but managed to catch herself. She looked behind and saw a large bit of decking that had been what hit her. She grabbed onto it with both hands and tried to pull herself up. She struggled with it, but her hands kept slipping on the wet wood. Finally, she got the idea to try and slip her leg up first for leverage.

It took long minutes for Mary to finally scramble up on the bit of decking. She lay there shivering on the makeshift raft, numb from the cold. She could barely lift her head to see the final demise of the ship.

Bits of the hull were still intact, but massive holes allowed the sea water to rush in. Bodies floated everywhere around her. Mary didn't see anyone else that seemed to have made it out alive. She prayed her parents and sister were on the other side of the ship.

That hope went away as the bow of the ship dipped into the water and the whole ship spun around. The stern came close to knocking Mary from the bit of decking, and the massive propeller still turned slightly as it slipped back under the water. She saw the name of the ship scrawled across the back as it slipped under, and had to laugh at the absurdity of it: 'The Sainted Mary'.

Mary sat up on the decking, being careful not to rock it too badly. She didn't think she would be able to pick herself up again if she fell back into the water. Debris and bodies floated everywhere, but she didn't see another living soul. No sign of her parents or sister. No sign of anyone that still drew breath.

Mary couldn't stop shivering. She sat there, tears streaming down her face. She found herself lost in the middle of the ocean, with nothing and no one to help her. The storm that had raged just minutes before, passed by as if it had never been there. The sea calmed.

Mary saw a book floating by and grabbed at it. It was a Bible like the one she had seen in the drawer of her nightstand. She didn't really believe in God, but held on to the Bible with all the strength she had left. Maybe God was real, who's to say. If He was, why wasn't He helping her? She couldn't imagine any god that would take away a little girl's family the way He had. She lay back on the decking to close her eyes and cry, only for a minute.

Chapter Two
The Widows Platform

I never liked heights—until I realized falling was the point.

Mary woke, her head throbbing. Even through closed eyelids the sun hurt her eyes. Mary lay there, trying to make out what was going on. She lay on her back, that much she knew. Sand? She was on a beach. How had she ended up there? The shipwreck. She'd been in a shipwreck. That much she could remember. She forced her eyes open, wincing at the bright sun.

Bright blue sky greeted her, mocking her with its cheeriness. How long had it been since the storm? Mary couldn't be sure. Her hearing was muffled, but she thought she could hear a distant screaming. She tried to move, but every muscle in her body ached. She groaned, her throat felt like sandpaper mixed with turpentine.

Movement in the sky caught Mary's attention. She saw several birds floating on the wind high above, too far to make out. Buzzards?

After another minute Mary managed to sit up and look around. She sat on a long white sand beach, with the ocean waves lapping gently at her feet. She pulled her feet back and slipped her boots off, then her soaked socks. She hated wet feet.

Mary looked one way up the beach and saw burning bits of wreckage from the ship dotting the beach. She also saw a few bodies, all lying face down in the sand. The other direction was the same. Mary heard the screams again and tried to stand, but her legs felt like jelly and she sat down heavily. She glanced up at the buzzards again. Ever circling.

"I'm not dead yet!" Mary yelled at them, shaking a balled fist in the air. "Go someplace else."

Something about the birds didn't look quite right, but her eyes were so blurry and dazzled by the sun she couldn't make out what it was.

Mary tried to crawl in the direction of the woman's screams, but her knee gave out. She'd twisted her knee once, jumping from a tree that was perhaps a bit too high. This felt like it did then.

"I'm coming," Mary hollered to the woman.

Mary tried crawling again, using her good knee. In the wet sand, she made little progress one-legged. If she was going to help the woman, she was going to have to endure a little pain.

Mary bent the bad knee and screamed. She thought she was going to pass out from the pain. Did people do that? There was no way Mary could get to the woman.

A shadow passed over her and her blood froze. Had the buzzards finally decided she would make a tasty snack?

Mary looked up and her jaw dropped open, staring dumbly at the flying figures. It wasn't birds that circled around, it was men. With wings. It wasn't like the aero-planes she'd seen on display on the long fields at Dorset. These were men, with the wings strapped directly on their back. Mary watched their movements across the sky as they dipped lower and lower. The wings caught the sunlight, dazzling her eyes with tiny bits of reflected light.

The first of the men landed and the metal wings folded almost immediately into a neat little bundle on his back. He reached for a small canister mounted on the side of a belt he wore and dashed to the closest of the fires. When he aimed the end of the canister at the fire and depressed a small knob on it, a great jet of liquid shot out, dousing the flames and the bits of debris. It took only seconds for the fire to be extinguished and then he moved on to the next.

Mary became aware of others landing near her. Two of the men grabbed similar canisters and rushed off to other fires, yelling something she couldn't quite make out. They worked their way down the beach, putting out the flames.

Mary looked around for the other man and found him standing right beside her, hands on hips and a wide smile on his face.

"What do we have here?" the man asked. A thick red mustache twitched under his nose. He squatted down in the sand beside her. "Don't be afraid, little one. I know I may be big and mean looking, but I'm really a teddy bear once you get to know me. At least, that's what my wife tells me."

Mary smiled at him despite her fear. There was just something about the soft way he spoke, and the redness of his mustache.

When the man slid the brass goggles he wore up onto the top of his head, Mary could see just how blue his eyes were. She thought they rivaled the sky itself.

"I'm Roland," the massive man said. He held out a hand. "And who might you be?"

Mary took his hand and he raised her up, though she winced when her knee twisted again. "Mary Stewart. Where am I?"

Mary was always told she was quite tall for her age, but standing next to Roland she felt dwarfed, barely reaching the man's navel. She had never felt so small in all her life. She shivered in her damp clothes.

"Well Mary, this is the island of Staria. And just how did you find your way here?"

Mary started to speak, but stopped. What had happened? Her

memory of it all was still fuzzy. "I think there was an explosion on the boat. Please, I heard a woman screaming, over there."

Mary pointed in the direction where she had heard the screaming, and Roland caught the attention of one of the other men, who ran to investigate.

"Don't you worry none, we will take care of it. So, little one, do you think you can walk on that nasty knee of yours?"

"I think so."

Mary took a step and almost collapsed, but Roland caught her, sweeping her up into his arms as if she weighed nothing.

"Come on with me. You need tending to. My Alice, why she is a lovely healer. She will fix you right up."

Mary tried to pay attention to everything at once as Roland carried her through the woods down a well-trodden path. After several minutes of walking, Mary got up the nerve to ask.

"The wings, on your back. How do you fly with them?"

Roland shrugged. "We use the air currents that swirl around the island to keep ourselves aloft, and there are heat vents from the volcano that makes up these islands. Is that what you meant?"

"I suppose. Do you think I could learn to fly them one day?"

"I don't see why not," Roland grunted. Mary liked the way Roland's mustache curled around into his mouth and he had to keep blowing it out almost like he was whispering. "You're kinda small though. You might have to wait a while before you do. Why, I bet my wings weigh more than you do."

Mary smiled up at him. She had a million questions about the wings. How they worked. How you controlled them. How you launched yourself into the air. But she felt tired. Somewhere along the journey, she fell asleep.

***

When Mary woke up, she lay in a comfortable bed, looking up at roughhewn timber that held up a ceiling of thin, plastered slats. A heavy quilt covered her and she was so hot she was sweating.

Mary pushed the quilt off and tried to stand, but a hand pushed her back down.

"Stay put child," a woman's voice said. "You need to do some more sweating."

The quilt was spread up over her again, and Mary saw the woman who had spoken. She was a tiny woman, no more than a few inches taller than herself. She had beautiful auburn hair that fell below her shoulders in a tight braid she kept pulling over one shoulder.

"Sweating?" It was the only word Mary could get out from under the stifling heat she felt.

"Yes child, you had a fever when Roland brought you in. Sweating is the best way to get it out of you. Don't worry child, it will break soon. I know you must be uncomfortable."

"Who..." Mary tried to sit up again, and again the woman pushed her down.

"Alice. I'm Roland's wife. Stay. That's an order. Or do I have to get the dogs to come in and lay on you? They are friendly enough but they smell something terrible."

Mary smiled. "I will stay, if I can have some water."

"Yes, I suppose you are thirsty. Been here sweating for almost two days."

Two days? Mary glanced around, remembering. The ship. Her parents.

Alice shuffled from the room, carrying a small chamber pot with towels and other things.

Mary lay there wondering if anyone had gotten off the ship.

Surely, they had to be here someplace. If she had made it this far, there had to be others. So many questions rattled around in her head it hurt.

Mary heard heavy footfalls coming toward her and looked to the door. Roland stepped through, his massive frame filling the doorway.

"Yer awake. Good." Roland stepped through the door and sat carefully beside her on the bed, handing over a glass of water. "Drink slow, you ain't had much since we found you."

Mary sipped at the cool water, almost gagging. A few sips and her throat started to clear itself. "Where are the others?"

"What others?" Roland asked.

"From the ship. Survivors. The woman I heard on the beach when I woke."

Roland looked toward the ceiling. "Just you, little lass. Lots of bodies. Sorry little one."

"The woman?"

Roland grabbed the water glass when it grew unsteady in her hand. "She lived a time. But her injuries were too severe. We buried her with the others."

Mary grabbed at a chain around her neck, and the locket that hung from it. "These people, did you see them among the dead?"

Her world fell apart. Mary was shipwrecked someplace far from home, her parents were gone, her older sister as well. As far as Mary knew, she was all there was, except for Beatrice back in London.

Roland took the locket from Mary and fumbled with his big fingers until he got it opened.

"Sorry," he said, passing the locket back.

Mary looked at the pictures inside. They had gotten wet and the layers had separated, and there were tiny crystals underneath the glass. With the pictures destroyed, Mary didn't even have that to remind her of them.

Mary felt tired again, despite the heat of the room. She laid back on the soft pillow and closed her eyes. She felt Roland move from the bed and clunk his way across the room.

"You rest up child. You will feel better on the morrow."

***

Mary's eyes snapped open. The heavy quilt had been removed, replaced with just a thin blue blanket. She sat up, throwing her feet over the edge of the bed. She stretched her legs out and wiggled her toes; everything seemed to work. Mary looked around the room for her things.

In one corner, there was a writing desk made of burled wood with a matching chair. A small white oil lamp sat on the desk, burning low and throwing shadows over the wood paneling in the room. A book shelf stood opposite the desk with various knick-knacks and a few books. Beside that, was a ladder-back chair that held Mary's clothes and boots, all folded and tidy.

Mary walked across the chilly floor in her bare feet and slipped her clothes on, shedding the simple gown she wore. There was a moment of panic as Mary wondered who had put her in it. Mary pushed the thought aside and finished dressing.

Once Mary was dressed, she examined herself in a small mirror attached to the back of the closed door. She looked presentable at least, she just wished she could do something about her hair. She used her fingers to try and comb out the long brown locks, wincing at all the tangles she found.

There was a knock at the door. "Mary?"

Roland's voice boomed through the door. "Are you awake yet?

It's supper time and Alice reckons you should be up and moving now. You should eat something."

Mary opened the door and jumped back, once again surprised by the imposing bulk of the man. His size seemed unnatural.Mary wondered how the wings she had seen on him had ever kept him aloft.

"I'm starving," Mary told him. "It feels like I haven't eaten for days. Oh, I guess I haven't."

Roland led the way down a narrow hallway into a main room with a long table at one end. The table was filled with all manner of food that smelled wonderful.

Mary sat down and reached for a plate, then froze. "Umm, do you say prayers or anything? I don't normally, when I'm home."

Home. Was she ever going to see it again?

Alice smiled around the steaming hot bowl of potatoes in front of Mary. "Eat your fill. No god rules this house. We did our work. If anyone should be thanked, it should be us thanking ourselves."

Mary didn't quite know what to say to that, so just grabbed a plate and started filling it. She wasn't even sure of some of the items, but grabbed them anyway, covering the whole mess with a layer of thick brown gravy.

The three of them ate in silence, mostly with Roland and Alice watching Mary the whole time so she felt like an animal under inspection.

"So, when is the next boat to the mainland?" Mary wiped her chin free of gravy and bit into a yeast roll.

Roland and Alice exchanged looks. Alice shrugged and nodded at Roland.

"No boats come here lass. Dangerous reefs circle the islands. Most know to stay away, I reckon. The ones that come close almost never come close enough to see with a spyglass. That's how we want it, though." Roland reached over and thumbed a bit of gravy from Mary's cheek.

"Never? But how do you get to the mainland? It's the wings, right? You fly there? I bet that's a hoot and a half."

Roland shook his head.

"Mainland is hundreds of miles away. I'm not even sure how far. The wings would never make it that far. No hot air currents, you see. No strong ones anyway. Three generations on this island and no one has ever left. We came here to get away from all the hustle and bustle. We cut all ties with the mainland. We grow what we need, or we make it. No one ever comes here. That is, until you. You're something of a celebrity here. Everyone knows about you and can't wait to hear your story."

Mary let that sink in. She knew what it meant, but had to say it out loud to make it real. "So, I'm stuck here? But, I need to get back to London. My baby sister is there. She is all I have left now. Now that..."

It felt like a heavy hand had reached into Mary's chest and grabbed hold of her heart, her words hung heavily in the air. She felt like she could almost have reached out and grabbed them and stuffed them back into her mouth. Mary had to find a way back, there had to be something she could do.

"Don't you have boats here?" She tried to sound hopeful.

"Aye, lass. But nothing the size needed to make it across the ocean. We can travel between the other islands, but no further. And we just don't have the resources to make anything big enough to travel to the mainland, or even close."

Mary leaned back in the chair and let that sink in. She was stuck here, wherever here was.

"What am I going to do? Where will I live?" Mary had even more questions than before.

Alice looked at Roland and cocked her head questioningly. Roland nodded back and then spoke. "If you would like, Alice and I would like you to stay with us. We have this big house, and no children. I know it doesn't look like much to someone who is used to the fanciness of London, but it is comfortable."

Mary looked around the room. She loved how it all looked; cluttered and comfortable. She thought she could live here. It would take her some time to adjust, but she could live here.

Mary nodded. "I'd like that, if you wouldn't mind."

Alice smiled and jumped up, walked around the table and gave her a big hug. "Thank you."

Roland stood and grabbed a wrapped bundle from a table in the corner of the room. He came back and handed the bundle to Mary.

"Do you have your words," Roland asked.

"Huh?"

"Can you read and write?"

"Oh, yes. I am twelve after all. I had a tutor who came daily to the house. My penmanship is quite advanced, so my tutor says."

Mary unwrapped the bundle and found several blank notebooks and quills. She looked at Roland questioningly.

"I figured, you know, you could maybe start a journal about yourself. I will get you some ink in the morning. When I was little, about your age, I found that keeping a journal helped me deal with some things very similar to what you are going through. I'm not saying that I understand exactly how you feel, but..."

Mary sat the bundle down on the table and gave Roland a hug. Her arms didn't even reach around his massive body.

"Do you have a school here?" Mary wanted to learn all about the island she was going to be spending her life on.

"We do. I reckon you will want to be going then?"

Mary nodded. She hoped they didn't think she was crazy for actually *wanting to* go to school.

"So be it. All done eating then? Let's get you washed up and into bed. Looks like you could still use a bit of sleep. We will talk more in the morning."

Roland took her hand and started to lead her back down the hall, but Alice grunted for attention behind them. They turned around Alice walked up to Mary and looked her in the eyes. Mary could see a bit of sadness behind them.

"You know, it's perfectly alright to cry for your parents. If you felt the need."

Mary thought about that for a moment. She felt sad, but for some reason it just didn't feel like she was ready to cry. Not yet anyway.

"I'm fine," she shrugged, and turned back down the hall. Why didn't she feel like crying?

Chapter Three

A Sky for Borrowing

*The clouds didn't care who I was. They
only asked if I was coming.*

Mary woke the next morning to the smell of bacon and was up
in a shot. Despite the giant meal she'd eaten the night before, she
was beyond starving once again. Growing girls needed their nour-
ishment. She bounced from the bed and ran down the hall. Alice
was just putting a plate on the table when Mary arrived .

"Have a seat. You have a big day ahead of you," Alice said.

Mary cocked her head in question.

"Roland is going to take you into town to get you enrolled in
school. I think you are going to do a bit of shopping today as well.
You need clothes. Can't go around in the same old stuff every day."

Mary dove into the bacon and fried eggs. There were more of
the yeast rolls from the previous night, along with fried potatoes
and milk to drink.

Mary had a thought. "I... I don't have any money to pay for everything."

Alice stopped and looked at her. "Well then. What can we do
about that, hmm? I suppose, since you have no money, that you
could do some odd jobs around here. Let's call them chores. You
do these chores, and we will call it even for whatever you might
cost us, OK?"

Mary smiled. "I wouldn't have it any other way."

Mary was sopping up the last of the eggs with a roll when Roland came in, carrying a bundle of wood under one arm. He dropped the wood beside the hearth and looked at her.

"Are you ready?"

Mary nodded and jumped up from the table, running toward the door. She was eager to see the town, eager to see anything really.

"Hold it, missy. Seems we have one of these chores we discussed," Alice said. "I think all these dishes need to be cleared."

Mary turned to help, grabbing the utensils and throwing them into the sink. She scraped the scraps into a small dish Alice pointed out.

"What do I do with this?" Mary asked, looking around for a trash can or something similar.

"Ah, well. This is where you come across another of your chores. Come with me lass." Roland led the way outside.

Besides a few blurry minutes on the beach and a half-remembered walk to the house, Mary really hadn't had a chance to see much of the outside at all.

The house sat in the middle of a large patch of well-manicured grass that ran right up to massive trees that surrounded the whole property. The trees stretched high into the sky, perhaps 100 or even 150 feet , seeming to touch the clouds.

Roland called out to Mary as he disappeared around the side of the house. Mary carried the scrap bowl around and saw a big dog sitting on top of a dog house. The dog hopped down and walked up to her. For just a moment she was frightened. Standing on all fours the dog looked her right in the eye, but it seemed to smile at her with a goofy look on its face.

"Is everything on this island so big?"

Roland laughed. "This here is Jake. Not sure what kind of dog he is. Mutt, I guess. Dumb too. Built him this nice big house so he wouldn't get wet in the rain. He ain't even stepped foot in it. Prefers sleeping on top. Durn fool."

Mary stuck her hand out tentatively and Jake ignored it, instead putting a giant paw on her chest and pushing her down to get at the food she carried. Mary laughed and stood, brushing herself off as best she could.

"He's going to be your responsibility. You gotta feed him and make sure he doesn't have any burrs in his fur. He likes to roam, just call his name though and he will come running."

"Helo Jake," Mary scratched the dog behind his brown ears. The dog grunted and returned to his food.

Once the bowl was empty, Jake lost interest and rushed off to the woods, baying like a hound dog Mary had once met. She picked up the bowl and rushed it inside while Roland waited.

***

The pair walked for a while through a shady grove, passing a few houses along the way. From time to time Mary would see faces peeking from windows.

"Don't pay them no mind, they are just interested. You're new, and not much new happens here. Why, I bet by now everyone on the farthest island knows of your arrival."

Mary wasn't sure she felt comforted by his words. "How far away is that?"

"Forty-five minutes, if you have a nice tailwind. I bet every messenger on duty has carried word of you."

"You carry messages with the wings?"

Roland nodded. "Yep, fastest way. Besides, how else would we get there?"

Mary shrugged. "Boat?"

"I told you, we have a few boats, slow and not very big. Resources on the islands are not great, so we have to watch them carefully. A boat would just take too much."

They walked on in silence, with Mary staring wide-eyed at the houses and the people staring back. Mary started to notice the houses were growing closer together and soon found herself standing on top of a small hill overlooking a town that stretched off into the distance.

Mary hadn't expected such a large place. She just always figured islands were small. From the top of the hill Mary couldn't see the edge of town on the farthest side. In the distance, however, she could see a single mountain that reached into the sky, its peak hidden in the clouds.

"What's that called?" Mary asked.

Roland looked up to where Mary pointed. "Devil's Lair. It's an ancient volcano. They say that is why this island exists. And why we have such strong up-currents for flying. The town there is called Hardyville."

***

Once they reached Hardyville, Roland turned to Mary. "Go on and explore some. I've got a bit of business to take care of."

Roland pulled a pocket watch out and held it up to his ear, smiling. He handed the watch to Mary. "Hang on to this for me. We will meet back here in one hour, OK?"

Mary nodded as Roland turned to leave. She didn't really want to be left alone there, but she didn't want to argue with the big man either. She turned in a circle to get her bearings and fix the place in her mind. Mary started walking down the main street, looking in shop windows. Smells from a bakery drew her across the street, peeking in the window.

The baker had stacked layer upon layer of cakes and pastries in the window for display. Mary was glad she didn't have any money or else she would become quite fat in a very short time. Did they even use money here? Surely, they did, but what kind? Mary added that to the ever-growing list of questions to ask Roland and Alice later.

Mary walked on down the street and stopped in front of an unusual shop. In the display window, all manner of mechanical gadgets whirred and popped or crawled along. She couldn't resist going in, even if she didn't have money.

A tiny bell tinkled over the door as Mary pushed it open and a bespectacled man peeked over the counter at her.

"Yes?" The man voice was high and reedy. "How can I help you today?"

The man stepped from behind the counter and Mary saw he was a little person. He wore a brilliant white shirt with a black leather apron thrown over it, covered in bits of shaved metal and grease.

"I'm just looking if you don't mind." Mary felt guilty about browsing.

"Of course, please have a look around." The little man walked around to the front of the store, his gait wobbling a bit from side to side. "You're her, aren't you? The one from the shipwreck."

Mary nodded, suddenly self-conscious. "I'm Mary," she said, sticking her hand out. "Pleased to meet you."

"Melvin Arnest. Sorry to hear about your family, dear."

Mary nodded to him. It still didn't feel real. What was wrong with her? Why hadn't she felt anything?

Mary roamed through the low shelves, wondering at what half

the items even were. Some of them didn't make any sense at all, but still they were fun to look at.

"All hand made by me," Melvin said. "Oh, I guess most of it isn't very useful. But sometimes you just have to have some fun little things. Take this, for instance."

Melvin reached for a small wooden box on the shelf and opened it. Inside was a small pocket watch. The outer case of the watch was gilded in gold and carved with the scene of several gliders banking around a tall pole. The face was ivory, with dark numbers recessed in.

"It's a very beautiful watch. What scene is this on the back?" The watch was very light in her hands.

"Oh, just a general scene from the glider games."

"Glider games?"

"Each year, all the glider pilots get together from all of the islands and have competitions for bragging rights, and some monetary awards as well. Sometimes families will even wager against a pair of wings they covet of another family's."

"There are more gliders? I've only seen the four. Roland of course. They look like grand fun, to be up in the air like that."

"I'm sure they are. I can't even pick the darn things up."

"I would love to try them one day if I am still here."

Melvin nodded, but didn't meet her eyes. Mary knew what that meant.

"What did I say?"

"Nothing my dear, it's just... Females don't normally fly gliders. None that I have ever known, as a matter of fact."

"Is it forbidden?" Mary could feel her ire rising. Even on an island in the middle of nowhere it seemed that females were second-class citizens. Mary hated always being told, 'you're just a girl'.

"No idea, you would have to ask Roland that question. Since I can't fly, I never thought to ask."

Mary turned the watch over in her hand again and saw the smallest of buttons on the side. "What does this do?"

"Push it," Melvin said, smiling.

Mary did, and the watch face popped out of the case and flipped around, showing a wheel with tiny writing on it.

"See my dear, not just an ordinary watch. This one can tell you your fortune."

"I remember father warning me away from the Gypsy's who would try and tell people's fortunes. He said that type of thing wasn't possible."

Melvin shrugged. "Maybe; maybe it is just for a bit of fun. Try it. Press the little button on the side."

When Mary pushed the button, the dial spun clockwise with a high whirring noise, and tiny little clicks she could barely hear. When it stopped, she glanced at what it said. 'You will make a friend today'.

Mary pushed the button once again to see what it would say next. It didn't do anything.

"Oh no," Mary said. "Did I break it?"

"Of course not, dear. You already got your fortune told for today. I guess you will have to try it again tomorrow."

Mary handed the watch back, but Melvin held his hands up. "You keep it, my dear."

"Oh, I couldn't. I have no money to pay for it."

Melvin smiled at her. "I wasn't asking for money. Think of it as a gift, my way of helping out a young woman who currently has little in this life."

Mary didn't know what to say. She knew she shouldn't accept the gift straight out, but she really wanted the pretty watch with the flyers on it. She looked around at the dusty shop with cramped shelves. She remembered the deal she had made with Alice that morning.

"OK, on one condition: you let me come in and work it off, here in your shop. I can sweep floors and dust the shelves. It looks like they need it."

Melvin reached up and scratched his chin. Mary could hear the rough whiskers bending back and snapping under the tinkerer's rough hands. "Fair enough. As long as Roland agrees. I will have a talk with him. But until it is decided one way or the other, please keep the watch."

"Thank you." Mary hugged the short man. "I really should get back outside. So much I want to see."

Mary turned the door knob, but Melvin stopped her.

"There are usually a bunch of kids your age that hang out at the park. Two streets down and one over. Maybe it is time to go make that new friend?"

Mary smiled at him again. "Maybe I already have?"

Melvin blushed. "Go, be a kid and explore."

***

Mary walked down the street, the new watch tucked safely away in a pocket. She checked the time just to be sure. She still had half an hour before she was to meet back with Roland.

Mary found the park with little effort, enjoying the way the tall trees seemed to block out the whole town just as if she stood in the middle of a dense forest. Mary heard yelling coming from down a small path and decided to follow it. When she got there, she frowned.

Three kids were surrounding a smaller boy, pushing him back and forth between them. Mary didn't even think before she yelled out.

"Hey, leave him alone!" Mary pushed one of the bigger boys out of the way and picked up the smaller boy from where he had fallen.

"Stay out of this," a boy with sandy blond hair said. "This is none of your business."

"I tend to make it my business when three bigger jerks are bullying someone smaller than them." Mary stepped right up to the boy, even though he was a good three inches taller.

The blond boy sneered. "He's just a scrub, not even worth your effort.'

Mary didn't know what a scrub was, but the tone the boy used did not sound nice at all. Someone needed to stick up for the smaller boy. Right at the moment, he had no one, and it reminded her of her own situation. Mary had no one left either. Well, she was going to be the boy's 'someone'.

Mary wasn't sure what happened then. Maybe the events of the last few days had finally caught up with her. It was like something else took over. Mary balled her fist up and swung at the blond boy, sure she was going to miss. She felt the crunch under her fist when she connected with the boy's nose. Crimson red squirted out onto the boy's white shirt. She held her ground, expecting him to retaliate, but instead he ran down the path crying, his cronies following close behind.

"You shouldn't have done that, but thanks." The boy Mary rescued brushed himself off. "I think you've made an enemy today. That's Eric Dane, he comes from one of the top families here. You're that girl, the one from the shipwreck."

Did everyone know of her predicament?

"Yes, that's me. Mary Stewart." Mary stuck her hand out.

"Hubert Donovan, from Pulltree," he said, taking her hand.

"I didn't want to make any enemies. I just hate bullies."

"Eric and his gang are the worst kind. I think he might leave you alone though. I'm not sure anyone has ever actually stood up to him before. Did you see the look on his face?" Hubert laughed and stomped his foot happily.

Mary was miserable, sure she would never forget that look. It was the first time she'd ever hit anyone, and was pretty sure it was going to be her last.

"Look, I really should be going. I'm sure I will see you around?" Mary turned back down the path that would take her out of the park to go meet with Roland

"You bet."

***

Mary made her way out of the park and up the streets, back past the tinker's shop, and to the corner where she was to meet Roland. He was already there talking to a man who looked rather displeased. When Roland saw Mary coming he silenced the man with a word and walked away, pasting a smile across his face.

On the way back to the house, Mary told Roland about everything that happened. Roland was quiet through the retelling.

"I heard a bit of a different story about it. That man you saw me with, that was Eric's father. He spun quite a different tale indeed. But I believe your version, even before I heard it. The Danes think they are better than everyone else. His son is a little snot who needed to be put in his place, truth be told. Having said that, I'm a bit disappointed in how you handled yourself."

Mary understood what he meant, she was disappointed in herself as well. She could have handled everything so differently. "I'm sorry. I just don't know what came over me. And I will tell Mr.

Dane I'm sorry as well."

"You will do no such thing. Just try to watch your anger in the future. Eric's father can make life pretty tough here if he wanted to." Roland slipped a hand around her shoulders. "Come on, let's hurry up and see what dear Alice has cooked us up for lunch, shall we?"

Roland sprinted down the path, carrying his bundles. Mary took off after him, doing her best to keep up with Roland's giant strides.

Chapter Four

The Engine Keeps Singing

If it hums, it's still alive. Same goes for people.

Two months passed, and Mary was still happily working at the tinker shop. Melvin had been showing her how to fix things, and even how to make a few little gadgets and such to sell in the shop. He said he had never seen anyone take to tinkering the way she had.

Mary heard a commotion outside. Like everything else, news traveled fast in the town. Mary saw Hubert rushing up the street and then he hurriedly pushed the door open. She could tell by his face that something horrible had happened.

"Mary, you need to come. Roland has had an accident." Hubert said.

Mary dropped the bell she had been dusting and cursed under her breath.

"Is he OK?"

Hubert shrugged. "They are just getting him to the clinic. Go to him, I will run and tell Alice."

Mary looked back at Melvin, a pleading look in her eyes. He wiggled his fingers toward the door. "Go child, be with Roland. Take the rest of the day."

Mary sprinted out the door and down the street. Already a crowd gathered outside the clinic as she pushed her way through to the door. She saw Eric and his father smirking as she went in.

Roland sat up in bed, grimacing from pain. It was obvious from the odd angle that his right leg was broken in several places.

Mary rushed up and wrapped her arms around his chest.

"Easy girl, still a bit sore."

"Hubert has gone to get Alice. What happened?"

Roland shrugged. "Stupid accident is all. Was trying something new with the controls, they slipped out of position and I dropped. Guess it's a good thing I wasn't that high up. No one will tell me if the wings are OK."

"They are fine, I'm sure." Mary knew what the wings meant to the big man. He would rather lose a leg than the wings. "Let's just focus on getting you better."

"I agree," a woman in a white coat said. "Your convalescence is going to be a lengthy one. I'm going to need to set the leg of course, but I might need to put pins in as well to keep the bones in place as they heal."

"And then I can get back to flying?"

The woman pinched her face up. "I shouldn't think so. You're such a big fellow and the leg is going to be much too weak to support any kind of safe landing. There is a small chance, but I really doubt you will fly again."

Roland lay back on the bed, covering his eyes with an arm. "What am I gonna do?"

Mary put a hand on Roland's arm. "We will worry about that when the time comes."

The door opened behind them and a worried looking Alice rushed in. Mary couldn't miss the hushed whispers that followed her in from outside.

"Durn fool," Alice said. "Always gotta be playing at something. I told you something like this would happen one day."

"I'm fine dear," Roland said. "Thanks for asking. It was just a silly accident."

Alice laid a hand on Mary's shoulder. "Why don't you go on back to the house. Not much you can do here. Doc will fix him up right. It's not the first time this old fool has had to be patched up."

Mary nodded and gave Roland a quick hug, careful not to squeeze too tightly.

Mary could feel her face heat up when she walked outside. Everyone's eyes were on her.

"Is he OK, child?" someone asked from the crowd.

Mary nodded and smiled. She didn't want to give too much information, especially with Eric standing there. The crowd started to shuffle away, until Eric spoke up with a loud voice.

"I guess his own brand of clumsy finally caught up with him." Eric stepped in front of Mary and blocked her from leaving the stairs. "I've always thought he was a bit of a clumsy ox. Much too big for flying."

"He's the best flyer I know," Mary retorted.

Mary did her best to keep her anger under control. She was helped along by the fact that the very center of Eric's nose had a small little bump in it where she had broken it. She stuffed her hands into her pockets, just in case, and tried to push past Eric.

"Dad says he is going to petition to get the wings." Eric smiled slyly.

"What do you mean?"

"Didn't you know? The wings are gifted by the people of the island, they belong to everyone. They usually stay in one family for years and years. Roland has no heirs. Dad's already petitioned the council to be awarded the wings. Maybe before long you will see me with them. Of course, they will need a bit of work. I doubt the big lummox has taken very good care of them."

Mary did her best to keep her temper under control, but there was just something about Eric that drove her crazy. And now he was talking bad about the man that had taken her in months before. Without Roland, she wouldn't have anything. She could feel her fists balling up despite her best efforts. Fortunately, Hubert saved the day.

"Come on," Hubert said, grabbing her arm and dragging her through the throng of people standing around. "I've got a few hours before I need to go back to Pulltree. Let's go back to the house."

Hubert and Mary had become almost inseparable ever since the incident at the park. Even the great dumb beast Jake had accepted Hubert as his own. Though the dog would accept anyone who gave him food, or a pat on the head, or even a casual glance in his direction.

They ran down the path to the house for a few minutes, then slowed to a walk.

"So, what's going to happen to the wings if Roland can't fly," Mary asked.

Hubert shrugged. "Normally they would just be passed down to a son. He doesn't have any so I guess they go back to the guild. Other families will petition for the right to have them. Eric's family most likely will win. Half of the guild is his family."

Mary didn't like the idea of the wings going to Eric's family. She would rather see them destroyed than see that happen. In truth, she would love to have them for herself. Roland had promised to show her how to fly when she was older. But the fact of the matter was, Mary wasn't family, and wasn't a pilot. And, she also wasn't a boy.

"Come on, let's go find Jake and chase rabbits for a while."

Mary nodded and they took off down the path again, happy for the distraction.

***

Several weeks passed by, quicker than Mary would have liked. Roland and Mary stood in front of the guild of fliers. Roland's leg was wrapped in bandages still, and had a brace around it to absorb the weight of his massive frame. It was clear to everyone though that he would never fly again. The leg was healing poorly, with a slight bend in it, and the doctor didn't seem to think it would ever properly support his full weight again without a brace.

The guild hall was a massive room, as befitted the most popular guild on the islands. Everyone wanted to be a flier assigned to security or the messengers, or just to fly among the birds. Each and every seat in the place was packed, with several rows of people standing against the back wall. They sat on one side of the room, at a single table. Across the room from them was another table with five people seated, all looking rather impatient.

Custis Dane, Eric's father, stood and cleared his throat to silence the whispers in the room. It only half worked. The expression on his face grew dark when he had to do it a second time. It was clear he was used to having what he wanted, when he wanted it.

"The petitions are in. Why do we have a delay?" Mr. Dane's words dripped with his impatience.

The guild master stood, brushing his red robes back. "Yes, yes. Calm yourself."

Mr. Dane sputtered, obviously not used to being spoken to this way.

The guild master turned his head toward Roland and Mary, offering a consoling smile. "Do you have any words before we rule on this?"

Roland stood slowly. "I do, if I could speak to you privately."

The guild master considered the request, then nodded. "Your standing in this guild is well known to all. I will allow a brief word."

Roland grabbed the walking stick beside him and made his way slowly across the floor until he leaned against the table and whispered in hushed tones with the guild master. Mary saw everyone strain forward, trying to hear what was being said. She tried herself, but couldn't hear a thing.

Mary watched, curious as everyone else in the room as to what Roland said. Once or twice the guild master leaned back away from Roland and scratched his chin, once even glancing over at Mary with a questioning look on his face before going back to converse with Roland once again.

The guild master grunted and shooed Roland away, then turned back to the other board members in hushed whispers. Roland went back to the table and sat down next to Mary, a smile on his face.

"What is the hold-up?" Mr. Dane asked. "I have work to do. If we could just dispense with these proceedings and be done with it."

The guild master stood again, silencing the man with a glance. Even a Dane would not go against the guild master, that much Mary had learned. The guild master looked at each junior member of the board and each nodded in turn. "It has been decided. Several petitions have been made to the guild for assignment of the wings, and an interesting proposal has hit the table from Roland himself. For now, our decision has been made. At least for the next few months, the wings will remain in the care of Roland Sallish."

A murmur ran throughout the room along with several protests as well, with Mr. Dane's being the loudest.

"This is outrageous!" he bellowed. "It is obvious to all that

Roland will never fly again. So, I don't really see the need to allow him to hang on to the wings any longer. What do you hope to gain by this?"

"Our decision is final," the guild master said. "I do not have to explain myself to you or anyone else, for that matter. If you or anyone else has a complaint, you need to file it through official channels. Good day."

Mr. Dane grew red in the face, obviously not used to being dismissed in such a manner. Before he could say anything though, the guild master and other members of the board filed out of the room, the door clicking behind the last member.

"What's the meaning of this," Mr. Dane turned his ire onto Roland, who was just turning to walk from the building.

Roland ignored him, hobbling along, and pushing Mary in front of him. "Just ignore him," Roland whispered. "He is upset. People say bad things when they are upset."

To make his point, Mr. Dane threw a pile of obscenities toward them.

Outside in the fresh air, Roland paused and took a deep breath.

"Are you OK? Want to rest?" Mary put a hand on Roland's arm.

"I'm fine, a bit tired perhaps. Let's make our way back home."

"Let me rent one of the carriages, at least."

Roland shook his head. "It's only a mile, my dear. I can walk that far. No need spending such money when we don't need to."

Mary started to protest, but thought better of it. She knew that now, with Roland not working, that things were going to be a bit tougher. She knew that they were going to depend on the small pay she got from the tinker's shop.

They made their way back home, only pausing once or twice

for Roland to catch his breath and drink some water from a small skin he carried around his neck. Mary could feel the eyes of everyone they passed on her.

Alice greeted them at the door, along with the smell of roast potatoes and vegetables.

"Dinner is nearly ready. Go wash up now."

Roland leaned over and kissed his wife on the cheek and whispered something in her ear.

Alice glanced over at Mary, a smile on her face. Whatever the two of them were up to, Mary had no idea what it was. She didn't like secrets, but understood that sometimes they were necessary, and could even be fun.

Chapter Five
Hallow Wings and Honest Lies

We all lie to stay airborne. Some of us just get better at it.

Mary's birthday came. She was finally a teenager. It had been four months since she came to the island. Alice said she was going to have a party for her later in the day, and had even invited some of her friends to come for a sleep-over. She didn't really expect anything big as far as presents go, she knew money was tight. Mary did have her eye on a nice sweater though, hand-made from nearby Eavin Island where they had lots of sheep.

Alice woke her early. Mary stretched in front of the mirror. She didn't feel any different than she did the day before, but she wasn't sure how a 13-year-old girl was supposed to feel in the first place. Maybe she already felt like one and didn't know it. Mary's mother had always told her she was mature for her age, whatever that meant.

At breakfast, Mary kept looking at Roland, who couldn't seem to keep from smiling. He was acting very strange; Mary had to know why.

"What's going on?" Mary asked.

Roland almost giggled, then went back to eating his eggs and ham.

Mary scrunched her eyebrows together and looked at Alice.

"He's dying to tell you about your present," Alice said. "I told him to at least wait until you were done with breakfast. I swear, he is just like a kid sometimes. You'd think he was the one turning thirteen."

Mary rushed through her breakfast, excited just by Roland's demeanor. She hadn't seen him like this in a while. Since his accident, he had been mostly a sullen so-and-so. This morning though, he was just brimming over with happiness.

Once Mary finished and dropped her dishes into the sink, Roland jumped up, wincing once from the pain in his leg. The big man grabbed his walking stick and headed to the door. As they were leaving, Mary noticed the wings were gone from their mounting bracket by the door. She asked him about it and he just shook his head quickly.

Mary followed Roland up the long path to a nearby launch-pad perched over one of the islands thermal vents. She'd been up there a hundred times before, but it never stopped amazing her at its beauty.

At 100 feet above sea level, it was one of the lower launch-pads, but also one of the most powerful. A platform had been built out of wood and metal over a natural indentation in the hillside. Sulfurous smoke drifted up and when Mary walked to the edge to peer over, the fart-smelling wind that rushed up ruffled her hair. It was from this point that glider pilots could easily launch their wings into the air and begin riding the thermals up and up until they could glide down over a long distance.

Hubert was there, and the guild master himself, along with a few of Mary's other friends. She also noticed Roland's wings propped against a carrier.

"What's going on?" Mary asked again.

Alice stepped forward, a tear threatening to fall from the corner of her eye. "If you want... I mean, Roland and I..." Alice couldn't get the words out.

"Oh, for God's sake woman," Roland started. "Such a sniffy woman. Mary, if you want, Alice and I would very much like to formally adopt you and make you our own daughter." Roland barely got the words out before his own voice cracked.

Mary was stunned. She didn't quite know what to say. "I..." She rushed forward and wrapped her arms around Roland, practically knocking him down from the effort. Alice added her own arms to the hug.

"Does this mean you accept, girl?"

"Of course! I would be honored to be your daughter!"

"Good," Roland said, pushing her back. "Then I have a present for you. Since you are thirteen and all. A person's thirteenth birthday is when these traditionally get passed down."

Roland pointed to the wings in their carrier. He reached into a sack and pulled out a brand-new harness and held it out for her.

Mary didn't know what to say. Was Roland really offering her his wings? Roland held out the harness for her and she slipped it on. She knew how to do it, had seen it a hundred times before when she watched Roland and the others do it.

"Is this why the guild allowed you to keep the wings?"

Roland smiled big then. "Of course. Even then I knew I wanted you to have the wings." Roland adjusted the harness, testing the fit. He smiled when he was happy, then slipped one of the brass altimeters on her wrist and gave it a tap. "So, are you ready to give them a go?"

Mary couldn't believe what she was hearing. "Now? I've never flown before, you know that."

"Have to start someplace." Roland pulled out a long cable from a receptacle mounted on the side-railing of the launch pad and attached it to the harness with a hook. The other end of the cable fed into a system of pulleys mounted on the side of the platform. "Now, these are gonna be a bit heavy at first, until you get used to them."

Roland hefted the wings from the carrier and slid them into place on the harness. Mary struggled to keep her balance, and, after a few tense moments, finally found the sweet spot to keep herself upright.

"Now," Roland said. "We are going to slip you out into the thermals. Just relax and feel what the wings want you to do. Don't worry, the cable will keep you from flying away. And if you lose control and fall, it will catch you easy. I can feed out or bring in cable as needed. Just try to keep the wings level for now. Ready?"

Mary nodded, suddenly terrified of the prospect, but she couldn't let Roland see she was scared. For the last few months, this was all she had wanted to do.

Roland and the guild master grabbed either side of the wings and extended them. "Now normally these would extend on your command with a flinch of your back muscles, but you aren't strong enough yet. It will happen quick though. You will see."

Once the wings were extended, the pair of men moved Mary backward toward the edge until her feet were right on the edge. Roland caught her eye, questioning her readiness. She nodded.

Mary tried to push herself off, but something stopped her. She was scared. She wanted to do it, but there was that little piece in the back of her brain that kept her from taking that last step. She looked up at Roland and he smiled, then reached out and pushed her off the platform. For a moment Mary was in free-fall, but then the warm air caught her and she squealed. She had imagined what it would be like to fly, and now she realized that her imagination had failed miserably in this one respect. She knew in that instant that this was what she wanted to do, always. It was what she was made to do. It took a few seconds for her to find the balance point, but once she did she found it was an easy thing to float on the current. Roland allowed slack in the line as Mary drifted higher and higher. She could see the people below her, clapping and yelling out, but the wind rushed by her ears so fast she couldn't hear them.

Mary tested subtle moves that Roland had told her about all those times he spoke to her about flying. She found she could float around in circles or hover in place, or swoop down momentarily before she caught herself. Tears streamed from her eyes, but she wasn't sure if it was from the air rushing up over her, or pure joy. She realized it didn't really matter. She was flying.

Mary wasn't sure how long she drifted in place, but suddenly she was reeled in and she felt terra firma under her feet once again. It took a moment for her to find her legs. She looked up at Roland; he had the biggest smile on his face that she had ever seen. Even Alice was smiling, though with a touch of terror in her eyes.

"Oh lass, you did great. Like a duck to water. You were born for the sky." Roland unhitched her from the cable and slid the wings off her back, placing them back in the carrier.

Mary stood there on the ground, but barely felt it. "When can I go again?" The words rushed out in a blur.

"Every day, Mary. You are going to get tired of practicing."

"Never!"

Roland laughed and patted her back, pushing her down the path as everyone else followed behind. "Come on girl, you have a party to get to."

Mary took a moment to look back over the platform out at the sea. Somewhere across the water her sister was there. She wondered if her sister thought about her today?

Chapter Six
Smoke on the Horizon

You can't chase the future without setting
fire to something.

In short order, Mary was finally allowed to do solo flights, though Alice voiced her opposition quite vocally indeed. In the end however, Roland and Mary won out. Alice was always so forgiving.

Mary floated on a thermal, hovering almost in place, watching the land hundreds of feet below her. She saw something that caught her eye on the horizon. A ship. She followed the thermals until she could see the ship very clearly. However, she couldn't find another thermal to get any closer. Once away from land, the thermal currents were harder and harder to find, and Mary was inexperienced. She once got almost out of sight of the island before she was forced to return.

Mary was ready though. She drifted quickly down to the beach, landing lightly. She shrugged the wings from her back and rushed over to a giant pile of brush she had assembled just last week as part of a plan to attract any passing ships.

Mary pulled out a small flint lighter and clicked the button. Flame came to life and she touched it to the bits of fluff placed at the base of the bonfire. It flared to life, quickly spreading to the whole pile. She couldn't launch again to see if it was doing any good as there was no pad there. Mary would have to carry the wings at least a mile from where she stood to launch.

Once Mary was sure the fire burned bright, she hitched the wings up under her arm and started up the path that would take her to a launch pad. She very nearly ran to the launch spot, fixing the wings in position on her back. This was still the hardest part for her, but she was getting better. Her back grew stronger each day.

Mary stepped to the edge and reached out a hand, feeling the strength of the thermal, then stepped out into the open air.

The metal wings caught the rising air immediately and launched Mary up. Within seconds she was several hundred feet up before the thermal released her. She started a slow glide down, catching the smaller thermals she knew of along the way as she headed back to the beach. Mary saw a patrol circling the beach over the fire she had set, then quickly scanned the horizon. She could still see the ship, though it didn't look any closer than it had before.

They just have to see it.

Mary flew over the beach, gasping at what she saw. The signal fire had toppled over, lighting surrounding brush on fire, and it was spreading fast. The patrol of four swooped down and landed, each pulling the canisters lose from their belts.

Mary landed quickly as well. She didn't have any canisters but, perhaps, there was still something she could do. She watched as one of the men aimed his canister at the fire. When he released the tab, the great gush of liquid pushed him tumbling backward, end over end. She'd never seen that happen before and was amazed at the power the canisters had.

It took several minutes for the fire to be contained. The whole time Mary stood by, feeling guilty. There were homes just through a small patch of trees. If the fire spread to them then all could be lost.

One of the patrolmen turned and glared at her. "Did you set this?"

Mary nodded. No sense lying to them. "There was a ship on the horizon, I was trying to draw its attention."

"Whatever for, girl?"

"To get home. My sister still needs me. I'm the only family she has." Mary tried to hide the tears but it was no use, they streamed down her face, leaving damp trails in the soot.

"Look, I can appreciate you have a need to get home; we all understand that. But you have to be very careful with fire this time of year. As dry as everything is, it could spread very quickly to other parts of the island and wipe us out. It's happened before."

Mary nodded again. She had tried and failed.

Chapter Seven
Clock Hands and Promises

*Time breaks everything, but some things
break back.*

Mary stood on the launch pad, the brown leather messenger bag around her neck and strapped down around her waist. She took to delivering messages to the other islands six months ago, ever since Melvin's passing. She still missed him, and his tinker shop. His brother had no interest in keeping the shop open, forcing Mary to find other work. Fortunately, she scored a position with the messengers, although there were those that opposed her appointment.

Mary stepped out into the thermal, thrilling at the way it felt to fly. No matter how many times she did it, each time was like that very first.

Mary was in for a long haul today. She had to go to Pulltree Island. It could be a difficult journey because of the distance, but she had become adept at reading the thermals. She even held the record for flight time, much to Eric Dane's dismay.

The flight there was uneventful, but enjoyable just the same. Mary locked forward to seeing her friend, Hubert, so they could talk. She hadn't seen him for a week or more and really wanted to get his input on a plan she had.

After all of her messages were delivered, Mary hung her wings in a carrier and walked down the path toward Hubert's house. She hugged him as he invited her in.

"What's up?" Hubert asked.

"I have an idea about making long journeys with the wings. I'm just not sure how to put it into action."

Mary grabbed a piece of paper from Hubert's desk and started drawing out her plan. "Now, what I'm thinking about, is using the fire canisters the patrols use, and modifying them somehow. I need to increase the pressure that is released to give me extra lift."

"You know that sounds crazy, right?"

Mary shrugged. She had to try something. Each day that passed was another day away from her sister. Despite how much she loved the islands, and flying, she'd started to get antsy to get back to Beatrice. "I have to try something. Are you in or out?"

"What do you need me to do?"

"Your father is on the patrols, yes?"

Hubert scrunched his eyebrows together suspiciously. "Yes."

"I need you to find a way to get your hands on some of the canisters for testing. I've worked out a nozzle that should fit on the canisters, but I need to make some test flights to get it right."

"I think I can do that; or, at least, I know where they are stored. We will have to sneak in. Show me what you are going to do."

Mary drew a set of wings on the paper. "Now see right here? This area of the wings is always immobile, so I should be able to mount some canisters there, on each side. I will need some kind of trigger to open them." She drew the canisters mounted under the wings, and a line running up around the harness.

"I'm thinking I can release the canisters for added lift if I can't find a thermal, and then just fly up as high as I can go, so I can drift further. I should be able to make it to the mainland that way." Mary put the pencil down. "If I'm lucky."

"And if you're not?"

Mary shrugged. "Let's not think about that part yet, OK?"

Mary folded up the piece of paper and slid it into a pocket. "So, again I ask: are you in or out? You could get into trouble if we get caught stealing the canisters."

"If you can risk your life on this foolhardy scheme, I can risk a bit of time in jail."

"We are kids, what is the worst they can do?"

Hubert answered for her. "They can take your wings."

Mary shrugged the thought of losing her wings aside; she had to try, for Beatrice.

***

Night came, and Hubert and Mary made the short trek to the storehouse. They were both as scared as they could be. Never in all of her flights had she felt such fear as when she crouched outside the low fence that marked the secure area. Mary didn't see any patrols or anything like that, but she knew they had to be there.

The two of them waited for what seemed an eternity before making their move. They climbed over the fence, and dropped down the other side, pausing again to listen. When no alarm was raised, they made their way as stealthily as two 14-year-olds could. Mary tripped over an exposed root and cursed as she banged her knee.

Hubert turned and hissed at her to be quiet. Mary swore his hiss was as loud, if not louder, than the noise she had made. She picked herself up and they continued on. She could feel the thumping in her chest. It truly felt like her heart was going to explode at any moment.

They made it to the door and tried the knob. Of course, it was locked. They had expected it to be, but still they had to try. There were a few high windows around the other side of the building: those were the target.

Around the building they went. The windows were higher than Mary could reach. Hubert got on his hands and knees, making a nice platform for her to crawl up on. Mary reached the windows then.

She placed her hands on either side of the window and gave an experimental push upward. She saw the chain connected to the window, but not in time. The chain was connected to a pin on the window, and when the window raised the pin dropped out. She tried to grab the chain before it snaked away up the window sill.

A loud ringing bell sounded inside. Mary pushed the window all the way up and pulled herself in, searching for the bell. It was mounted at the top of one wall, just out of her reach. She noticed the chain that had been released, slowly feeding itself into the bell as it rang. She grabbed the chain and held it in place and the ringing stopped. One problem down, but Mary wondered who had heard the racket. This time of night she hoped that everyone around had been in deep sleep. She wrapped the chain around an exposed nail beside the window to hold it in place.

Mary peeked out the window and saw Hubert trying to jump up to grab at the window sill. She grabbed his hand on the next attempt and helped him shimmy his way up.

After Hubert was in the building with her, he went in search of the canisters as Mary watched for any sign they had been heard. She didn't see anything that signaled they'd been heard.

Deep inside the building Mary heard a clanging and a short string of curse words.

"Quiet," Mary hissed.

"You be quiet."

There was more clanging and then Hubert appeared at her side with two canisters.

"What was all that noise?"

Hubert shrugged. "I knocked over a couple canisters. Empties I think."

"Did you pick them up?"

"No time," Hubert said, pointing out the window.

Across the narrow street Mary saw a light come on in one of the houses. She knew right then they had to get the heck out of there. She jumped out the window and waited as Hubert dropped the canisters down to her. Once they were both out, they ran across the small yard and over the fence.

The pair ran all the way back to Hubert's house, ditching the canisters in the shed before sneaking back in so they didn't wake his parents up. Once they got to his room, they both collapsed on the bed, exhausted from the run.

"I can't believe we just did that," Hubert panted.

Mary sat up, still shaking, finally able to catch her breath after the long run. "Fun huh?"

"You have a warped sense of what fun is."

Mary smiled at him and then things got weird. Hubert got this weird look in his eyes and before she knew what happened, he leaned forward and kissed her. Right on the lips.

Mary pushed him back. "Eww, what are you doing?"

"I'm sorry," Hubert said, scracmbling back to the end of the bed. "I just thought that..."

"What did you think?"

Hubert started to say something else, but apparently thought better of it. "Never mind."

"Come on," Mary said, pulling some blankets from his closet onto the floor to make a pallet for herself. "Let's just get some sleep, OK?"

Hubert nodded, happy to be off the hook for whatever that was.

Mary curled up on the floor while he took the bed. She started to think about how she could modify the canisters, and her first test flight as she drifted off to sleep.

Chapter Eight
Beneath the Wingline

The air's thinner up here, but so are the excuses.

It took a bit of work, but Mary managed to get the canisters back home with little trouble Keeping them hidden from Roland and Alice was the biggest trick. She had a small workshop out behind the house that she used for minor tinkering. It was one thing she got from working with Melvin in the tinker shop.

On her days off from her duties as a messenger, she sequestered herself away in the workshop. The big dumb dog kept a close watch, barking when someone would come close. Usually.

It took less time than expected to sort out the solutions to her canister problems. A bit of measuring here, drilling there, and some well-placed nuts or bolts did the trick. Or, rather, they did the trick enough. It would do for a test flight.

Still, she knew she wouldn't get another chance at a test again. Unless, of course, she could convince Hubert to steal her some more canisters. But she figured they would be watching the place pretty closely now. Mary attached the canisters to the wings and headed up to the launch pad. Mary was going to go to Pulltree Island to be with Hubert. He risked a lot getting the canisters with her, so she figured she would let him be there for the test.

***

Mary managed to make it to the distant island with no one noticing the canisters mounted to the wings. In hindsight, she figured she could have probably carried the canisters in her messenger bag like she had the morning she'd returned from her heist.

Hubert followed Mary up to the launch pad. He was silent, trudging behind her with worry.

"It's going to be OK," Mary told Hubert. "What could go wrong?"

"Do you want a list? Least of all is being caught with the stolen canisters," Hubert complained, but still carried the wings up to the launch pad for her.

Mary was used to carrying the wings now, but still she let him help all the same. He needed to feel like he was doing something. She could see the nervousness on his face. She couldn't really blame him; she was nervous too.

Mary strapped the wings into the harness on her back and grabbed the wire that would deploy the canisters, attaching it to the gloves she wore. She checked the brass altimeter on her wrist, gave it a slight tap to make sure the needle moved freely.

"Ready?" Mary asked him.

Hubert shrugged. "I'm just watching. Are you ready' is the question."

Mary had to admit, she was more than a bit nervous; she was scared. She didn't know what was going to happen. Anything? Nothing? Well, nothing ventured nothing gained.

Mary leaned in and gave Hubert a quick kiss on the cheek.

"That's for luck, nothing more," Mary told him firmly. "Don't read anything into it. It was just for luck."

"Sure, sure." The way he smiled though, Mary was sure he was already planning their future together.

Mary stood on the edge of the platform and stuck her hand out to feel the thermals. She closed her eyes and let her fingers sense the ebb and flow of the warm drafts. In the short time she had been flying she had learned much about them. Roland told her once that he thought she could read the thermals better than anyone, even him. It was almost like she could see the air somehow, know how it was going to behave.

Mary stepped from the platform and dropped a few feet before the thermal caught the underside of the wings and held her steady. She started a spiral pattern, rising up higher and higher.She was, perhaps, a thousand feet up when the thermal gave out. No time like the present. Mary angled the wings up a tad and set the outer sheets stiff to catch as much lift as she could. She pushed a plunger, releasing the canister lock.

The blast propelled her forward much faster than Mary had anticipated. She nearly lost control of the wings, fighting to keep them stabilized. She had never flown so fast, not even in a controlled dive. The wind tore at her eyes, making them water. Goggles. She need goggles.

Mary kept the angle of the wings steep as she climbed, timing the burn of the canister. The canisters gave out at just over sixty seconds. She chanced a look down.

The island was a tiny speck. It was hard to breath. Mary had to work her lungs extra hard just to get small breaths in and she was getting dizzy. When she glanced at the altimeter on her wrist, it read at nearly 10,000 feet. At first Mary thought it was the height but then she realized that the air was thinner up there, like the time she and Roland climbed the mountain. By the time they had reached the summit, both of them were having trouble breathing.

Mary still rose as the last of the canisters blew themselves out. Her vision blurred and it felt like she was going to pass out. She lost control of the muscles in her arms and they began to hurt. The wings wobbled and started to tilt downward.

Mary struggled to regain control. At the rate she fell, it would be mere seconds before she hit the ground. She had never moved so fast before. She twitched the muscles in her back, trying to deploy the braking flaps, but at this speed they wouldn't open. She managed to tilt the nose up some, hoping she could use friction to slow her pace, but that only managed to catch too much air.

The nose of the wings caught at the air and tossed Mary over onto her back. Her arms and legs flailed, trying to right herself. She had never been upside down either, though she had seen others do it. The wings started a free-fall tumble and she knew she was in trouble. Before anything, she had to gain control of her body. Mary had to right herself or she was just going to slam into the ground at terminal velocity.

Mary twisted her back, hoping to ease the wing tips around to catch the air. It didn't work, instead setting her in a faster tumble. As her view alternated between sky and quickly approaching ground, another idea hit her.

Mary worked her back muscles and the ailerons to get the nose of the wings pointed straight down. She had to squint into the air as her speed increased even more from the streamlined position she was in.

Slowly Mary tried to move the nose up a bit, hoping to catch just a small bit of air at a time, not to slow her decent, but to give her a shot at arcing downward rather than straight down. Just a bit of arc would save her.

Through teary eyes Mary saw the ground closer than she would like, making her work the wings harder still, pulling a muscle in her back. Slowly, though, the nose of the wings tilted and caught the air just as she hoped, less than a hundred feet from the ground. She angled herself toward the mountain and glided down the sloped face, giving herself more run-out room.

The tree line approached, but Mary was able to sweep the wings forward and catch the air once again, flying over the top of the canopy. She could hear Hubert whooping below as she flew over.

Mary still wasn't sure how she managed to pull herself out of it, but somehow, she did. Once her feet touched the ground near where Hubert stood, she stripped the wings from her back and collapsed onto the ground, nearly kissing it.

Hubert came running up to her. "What were you thinking? Don't ever do that again!"

"It was an accident. I wasn't quite sure how it was going to act. Didn't help I got dizzy while I was up there."

"Dizzy?" Hubert looked at her with concern.

"The higher up you go, the less air there is. I guess I went a bit too high." This was a problem that she needed to figure a solution to.

"So that's it then," Hubert said. "You can't make it back to the mainland like that."

Mary shrugged. There had to be a solution. Maybe she could use one of the canisters and pack it with air instead of the fire-extinguishing fluid.

"There is a way, I just need to work it out."

"So how far do you think you can glide once you get to maximum height?" Hubert picked the wings up off the ground and folded them.

"Dozens of miles at least without any thermals at all." That was a problem as well. Mary knew the mainland was at least a couple hundred miles away. She was going to need more canisters, and a lot of luck.

They started the short trip back to the launch-pad. Mary needed to get back to her little workshop and start on the modifications she would need.

"I still don't think this is a good idea." Hubert was shaking his head the whole time. "You have no way of knowing if you can make it or not."

"Maybe, but I have to try. Beatrice can't be without any family. She needs me."`

Chapter Nine

The Bones Beneath Brass

*It's not the wings that make you fly. It's the
bruises you earn landing.*

Mary cracked her eyes open and groaned. Today of all days
Mary did not want to get out of bed. Alice had other ideas though.
She bounded into the room. How did this woman have such energy so early in the morning?

"Come on sleepy-head," Alice said. "You can't sleep the whole
day away. It's your birthday, or did you forget?"

Mary didn't forget, she just chose not to accept it.

"You're fifteen now, and you have work."

"There isn't anything special about being fifteen." Mary pulled
the blankets up over her head again. The woman had to go away
or Mary was going to kill her. Unfortunately, Roland had other
ideas as well. She heard his heavy footsteps enter the room.

"Nothing special," he said. "Humph. You can compete in the
games now. I'd say that is pretty special."

Mary reluctantly got out of bed, stubbing her toe as she shuffled across the room to grab her fluffy robe. For early August, it
was a bit chilly.

"True, but do you really think anyone is going to let me?"

"Why wouldn't they?" Roland sat on the edge of her bed.

"Umm, because I'm a girl. Or have you forgotten that?"

"No rules against girls competing."

"No precedent for it happening, either. No one seemed to like it too much when I joined the messengers. I bet they really won't like me joining the games."

Roland shrugged.

It had been an uphill battle since that day. No one could legally have Mary stripped of her duties, but that didn't mean she would always have work. Some of the older people still refused to allow her to carry messages for them. Mary didn't really care, it gave her a chance to practice her flying or work on the canister problem.

"Scared, are you? Afraid the big bad boys will beat you in the games?" Roland smiled at her. He knew Mary was one of the best pilots around. Not that he would admit it, but she often saw it in his eyes.

Mary shrugged, perhaps the games would be fun. They were still several months away though. Plenty of time to practice. And she didn't have to put her name in the hat until the end of February.

"Maybe I will give it a try, just for laughs." Mary bunched her hair up in a ponytail and walked out of the room, leaving Roland sitting there.

"That's my girl," he bellowed out the room and then followed her to the table, his heavy feet clomping. His limp had almost disappeared, but still he wouldn't be able to fly. It was up to Mary to uphold the "family honor" as it were.

Mary ate quickly and dressed as usual. She still had deliveries to do, even if it was her birthday.

"I'm off to get some flying time in."

Mary grabbed her wings from the carrier and hiked the short distance up to the pad. Eric Dane was there, joking with some of his friends. His face soured when he saw her.

"What are you doing here?" Eric demanded.

"Work," Mary shrugged back. Since breaking his nose, the pair had barely spoken more than a few words at a time to each other. That suited Mary just fine. Eric was an arrogant bastard. Everyone knew it, even his friends, but his family controlled a large portion of the resources on the island, so everyone kissed his ass. That wasn't something Mary wanted to do.

Mary slid her wings up into the harness and tied them off, getting ready to step out into the thermal. Eric pushed her aside with a laugh and she jarred her knee sideways. She swore out loud and turned to face him, but he stepped out onto the thermal with his own wings, and her messenger bag.

Mary took off after him. That bag had her notebook with all of her drawings about the wing modifications. She couldn't let him have it.

Mary could hear him laughing as he dropped from the thermal and screamed downward to the island floor.

Mary kept her height and shadowed him from above, watching. She knew the thermals better than he, and could almost tell where he was going to have to turn.

Mary watched and waited, and when he had boxed himself into a single flight-path, she dove, quickly gaining on him. She flew with the sun at her back, so he never saw her coming.

Since her little test flight with the canisters, Mary had been practicing certain moves that she thought would come in handy. She closed in on him and twisted around until she flew upside down.

Mary timed it perfect and scraped right under his belly before he even knew she was there. She grabbed her messenger bag and gave it a tug, trying to dislodge it from his grasp. Her actions threw Eric off balance and he dropped suddenly, trying to regain control.

Mary knew he was in trouble then. There were no thermals

here to help him out. If he couldn't gain control he was going to crash. She just hoped he could keep his speed down.

Eric clipped a tree on his decent and it spun him around until he crashed down into a hedge. It wasn't a rough landing, but Mary knew he was going to be sore after it.

Mary wasn't sure what to do, so she aimed for a clearing close enough to land in. Eric wasn't hurt, but she knew he was going to be upset. She landed and plopped the wings from her back and rushed through the tight trees, looking for him. Mary heard him cursing long before she got to him.

"Are you OK?"

Eric stood there glowering at her and shaking. He slid the wings off his back and that's when Mary saw the bend in the center spine of them.

"The guild is going to hear about this, the magistrate too."

"It was an accident. Why did you take my bag anyway?"

Eric opened his mouth to say something, then snapped it shut, smiling instead. "I didn't take your bag. You attacked me, unprovoked. You know it is against the rules to come into contact with people in the air for this very reason. Who is going to fix these wings?"

Eric folded the wings as best he could with the bend in them and stomped off through the forest, heading for town. Mary knew she was going to be in trouble. Not matter what lies he told, everyone would believe Eric over her. Mary followed the trail she had forged through the brush and grabbed her own wings, folding them. She headed home. At least there, there was at least one person who would believe her over Eric.

Chapter Ten
Flight is a Kind of Memory

Every revolution is a story told in past tense.

When the magistrate came to get her the following day, Mary realized just how serious it was. He showed up at the door with two security men.

The knock echoed through the whole house. Roland went to answer it. Mary heard talking, but couldn't make out the words. Then the door shut and she heard footsteps coming into the living room.

"Mary Stewart?"

The magistrate was a balding man, hunched and old. But still his eyes held some quality to them that scared her.

"Yes?"

"I have a warrant for your arrest, along with a writ to seize the wings you have been using. There have been complaints about your actions. Causing one young man to crash land, and talks of illegal modifications to the wings themselves. And I have to say, you are now a person of interest in a robbery that took place several weeks ago."

Mary nodded and stood. She wasn't going to deny anything, but neither was she going to confess. There was a chance she could get out of this without Hubert getting in trouble with her as well.

The trio led her back to town and Mary was quickly thrown in a cell. She sat on the bench and tried to take stock of everything that had happened so she could explain her side of the story, even if no one was going to believe her. Instead, she fell asleep.

When Mary woke, it was near dark outside. She heard Roland's booming voice echo through the small building.

"There is bail for the girl, I wish to pay it," he said.

Mary wasn't sure where he had gotten the money. Even with her contributions they were barely scraping by.

Roland was led back to the cell. He stood there looking at Mary. She wished he would yell or rage, or something. Instead he just stood there looking at her, with that hurt look in his eyes. She had disappointed him. Time and again he had warned her about her temper, especially when it concerned Eric Dane. There was just something about him that rubbed her the wrong way.

The jailer released Mary into Roland's custody. The walk back to the house was a quiet one. She wanted to know what would happen to the wings; she'd seen them sitting in a carrier outside the jail house with a big lock on them. Roland would barely speak to her.

When they got back to the house, Alice had dinner on the table. That seemed to be her solution to everything: throw enough food at something and the problem went away. Alice was a great cook, but Mary didn't think that a pot roast was going to make this disappear.

Alice hugged her when she walked in. Mary could see she had been crying.

"I'm sorry," was all Mary said to her. What else could she say? Mary knew she messed up and there was no fixing it.

They ate in silence. After dinner Roland walked out the front door without a word. Mary started to follow but Alice held her back, shaking her head.

"Don't. He just needs to cool off a bit first dear. He doesn't hate you."

"I know."

Mary helped Alice clean up and then went into her room. She laid on the bed trying to sleep, but she knew it wasn't going to come to her. She needed those wings if she was going to make it back to the mainland. There was only one thing for it. Mary tried to talk herself out of it, but even as she grabbed the bolt cutters from her workshop she knew her mind was already made up. If Mary was going to get off this island, she need to take back the wings.

***

Mary made her way back to town and down the road to the jailers. The streetlights burned a bit too bright for her, but there was no way around it. She kept to the darker shadows as much as possible, hoping that the wings were still in the carrier.

They were, thank goodness. Mary broke the lock with the bolt cutters and slid the wings from the carrier. Now what?

Mary headed for the nearest launch pad, less than a mile away up a small hill. She jogged the distance in only a few minutes, adrenaline pumping through her. She had crossed the line there was no coming back from. Where was she going to go? For now, she could only think of one place.

Mary slipped the wings on her back quickly once she got to the launch pad, then stepped out onto the thermal. At this time of night it was weak, but still enough to give her the lift she needed. She spiraled upward, making up her mind once and for all. Mary headed off to Pulltree Island, and Hubert.

***

The trip through the darkness was scary, and difficult. Some of the thermals Mary had expected weren't even there. It was a cool night and a lot of the thermals were very weak.

It took her nearly an hour to go the ten miles to the island, having to double back to catch more currents often. Once Mary made it to Hubert's house, she said a little prayer, thanking whoever for helping her get there safe and sound. It made her wonder about the trip to the mainland. In the ocean, there were fewer thermals to contend with. Mary knew she was going to have to use multiple canisters. Her mind raced with a new solution. Maybe something that would allow her to discard the empty canisters…

Mary slung the wings off her back and crept through the yard, knocking lightly on Hubert's window.

It took a few minutes, but Mary finally saw his oil lamp blaze to life and he came to the window, rubbing his eyes.

"Mary?"

"Hey," Mary smiled. "Mind if I stay the night here?"

Hubert tried to process what Mary was saying as he scratched his head. "Sure, sure." He moved back so she could climb in the window. "What's this about?"

Mary shrugged. "Can we save it 'til morning? I'm beat."

Hubert nodded and grabbed a blanket from the bed and then laid down on the rug at the foot. "You take the bed. We will talk in the morning, OK?"

Mary nodded, too tired and emotionally wrung out to say anything else, or even protest his giving her the bed. She curled up underneath the covers, still warm from his sleeping. Within minutes she was asleep, her last thoughts of Beatrice as always.

***

Sun struck Mary's face, making her groan and roll over. She wasn't used to having the sun on her like this. Why was the sun on her? Mary popped up, instantly remembering.

Hubert sat in a chair, watching her from across the room.

Mary swung her feet over the edge of the bed and reached into the pocket of her slacks for the pocket watch. It was well past nine. She thumbed the little button and the dial slipped around to show her forecast. The dial spun around and around. When it finally stopped, Mary read it.

'Trouble lay ahead.' Too late, she thought, unless things got worse somehow.

Mary stretched, catching Hubert watching her. "What?"

He blushed and looked away. "Nothing. Want to tell me what happened?"

"Huh?" Mary pushed the crusty bits from the corner of her eyes, trying to clear the fog.

"Well, try starting with how you ended up knocking on my window at midnight."

"Oh, yeah." Mary didn't want to have to tell him anything, but figured she owed him an explanation.

Mary told him the whole story, not leaving anything out. He was silent for most of it.

"So, what are you going to do?" he asked.

Mary shrugged. What was she going to do? She had no plan, no idea how to proceed. She was a fugitive now. Surely, they knew it was her who took the wings. It didn't take a genius to add two and two and come up with Mary Stewart. Even Eric Dane could add that high.

"I dunno, I'm not ready to try the journey yet. Still need to make the extra modifications to the wings."

Hubert stood and crossed the room. When he sat down next to her, he put his hand on hers. "I know what you need to do, but you are not going to like it."

Mary allowed him to hold her hand. To be honest, she needed the contact. "What's that?"

"You need to turn yourself in."

Mary felt him tense up, like he was afraid she was going to hit him.

"You know I can't. If I go back now they are going to take the wings and do who knows what to me. This time I don't think there would be any bail."

"You can't live as a fugitive, Mary. The longer you wait the worse it is going to be. Give yourself up, give the wings back. Apologize."

Mary just couldn't. How could he even suggest such a thing?

"No way."

"But you have to. You can't live like this, where will you go. As much as I would like it, you can't stay here. My parents would get upset, and then turn you in. You know my dad patrols. Probably knows you are wanted by now."

Mary nodded. "Then I will go, I don't want you to get into any trouble." She stood and gathered up her things.

"Again? Go where?"

Mary stopped, she really had no place to go. Hubert was right, damn him. The only chance she had was to throw herself on their mercy and hope she didn't get put in a hole under the jail and forgotten. She thought about Beatrice. How was she going to get back to her? Surely, they wouldn't let her keep the wings. She was scared.

"Fine. You win. I will fly back and give myself up."

***

Hubert brought her some bacon and bread from the kitchen while Mary waited. They said their goodbyes and she climbed back out the window she had come in.

It was a bit of a hike to the launch pad closest to Hubert's house. Mary had plenty of time to think about things. Even with all that time, she still had no more answers to anything than she did before.

Hubert was right, of course. Turning herself in was the right thing - the only thing - to do.

Mary slid the wings into the harness on her back and extended them, then stepped out into the thermal. She circled there, letting the warm air wash over her face, drying the tears.

The trip back to Staria took longer than usual. But that was Mary's fault. She didn't want to end what could be her final flight. She was sure it was her final flight. The guild would have no choice but to strip her of the wings, and her status. They had never wanted to grant it in the beginning. They never said it to her face, but she heard the whispers behind her back: they didn't want to allow a female to fly; they didn't want a woman to break into their little club.

Mary swooped over the town, over the jailers. She could see people pointing up at her, some screaming at her, the wind whipping their words away. She saw Roland standing in front of the Magister's office, beckoning to her. Mary scrubbed speed and tilted the nose up, dropping down just a few feet from him.

A guild member came over and grabbed the wings from her back, unceremoniously folding them up and carrying them into the guild hall. Roland took her arm and led her inside.

"Everyone is waiting inside," he said.

"Why?"

"They were preparing to have a hearing on your fate, and that of the wings."

"How did you know I would come back?"

Roland shrugged. "We didn't. It is pure coincidence you came back now. Your fate was to be determined in-absentia. At least now you can speak on your own behalf before sentencing."

What was Mary to say? She did all the things she was being charged with. There was no excuse for that.

***

Turns out Mary didn't have to speak at all, nor would she have been allowed anyway. The Danes had exerted their influence over the guild. Mary was stripped of her pilot's license. The wings went to Eric Danes' family. Just like that. That smug look on Eric's face - she wanted to punch him until it was gone, but Roland grabbed her arm and ushered her out the door. Mary guessed he saw the look in her face. At least she was free. The guild didn't seem to care about much else but taking the wings from her.

They got back to the house and Mary had to endure the withering gaze of Alice. Why couldn't she just yell at her and be done with it? Her silence was killing Mary.

They all had a meal in silence and it made Mary wonder how long it would go on. She knew she had messed up, but how long was she to be punished? Even old Jake seemed to be giving her the silent treatment, even when Mary took him the table scraps.

Chapter Eleven
The Sky Remembers

The wind forgets you—but the sky never does."

Time passed by, and her misery continued. Mary couldn't take it anymore: Roland's disappointed stares, Alice's silence. She was always so happy before, and now she was a shell of her former self. She barely smiled now, and it seemed to rub off on everyone.

Mary had to find a way to get the wings back, if not for herself, then at least for Roland. Neither of them had a right to the wings, but Mary knew it would mean a lot to Roland to have them back in the family.

There was only one thing to do. Mary had to go talk to Eric and the rest of the Danes. She needed to find some way to convince them to let her have the wings back.

***

Mary made the journey up the long hill to the big mansion perched on top. They had their own launching pad off to the side. She walked over and put a hand out, feeling the thermal. She couldn't believe how strong it was. It must have been one of the strongest on the island. Mary imagined launching herself from the pad, eyes closed.

The image was ripped from her when someone spoke.

"What are you doing up here?"

Eric Dane and his father were crossing the long lawn toward Mary. Eric had that same smug look he always had. His father looked like he had just sucked a lemon.

Mary waited until they were in front of her, she wasn't going to yell across the yard. "I came to talk to you. I need the wings you have. I need to get back home and they are my only option."

"No," Eric's father said. Custis Dane shook his head, his heavy jowls shaking as he did.

"Please, if not for me, then for Roland. He is heartbroken I lost the wings. Even if I don't fly, I know it would mean a lot to him to have the wings forever in his carrier."

"Race me," Eric said.

"Huh?"

"Race me, next April in the annual games."

"Eric, I don't think that is a good idea. Those wings are right-fully ours."

Eric ignored his father's words, just like he did everyone else that went against him. "If you make it all the way through the games and we meet in the final round, and you beat me, then you can have the wings back to do with as you will."

"What if I lose?"

"Oh, there is no if about it. You will lose. And when you do, you will sign a document that says you will never fly again, will never touch a set of wings again. And..." Eric tapped his chin with a finger, thinking. "And you will work here at the mansion, in the kitchens washing dishes."

Custis snickered and set a hand on Eric's shoulder. "A fair shot. Anything less than making it to the final round and beating my son results in your loss."

Mary started to protest. What if Eric just threw the race somehow, never even made it to the final round? No, Eric was just arrogant enough not to do that. He would want the pleasure of beating her in front of everyone.

"Deal," Mary said, sticking her hand out. At first she didn't think Eric was going to take it, but then his father gave him a little shove. It felt like shaking hands with an eel.

"I will need to practice. Can I have the wings back? Until the races?"

Eric looked off into the distance for a moment, "No. I have a better idea. You will use my old wings, the ones you bent up. They umm, they still need to be straightened. I hear you like to tinker, I'm sure that is something you can take care of, yes?"

Mary knew it was the best she was going to get. She was confident she could beat Eric, no matter the wings. She'd done it once already.

"OK. Deal."

Eric called a servant over and had him retrieve the wings. They stood there in silence until his return. Even from a distance Mary knew the trouble she was in. The wings were bent much worse than she could have imagined. They wouldn't even fold up properly.

***

Mary made her way back down the hill, lugging the heavy wings along with her. They easily weighed half again as much as the wings she had been using. This was going to be a challenge. The first of many to come. First, she needed to fix the wings.

Once Mary got the wings back to her tiny workshop, she could get a better look at the damage. It didn't seem as bad as she had first thought. The spine was bent, but only a small amount. A few hammer strikes against the anvil and it was back in place.

The worst of it though, was a hinge hooked on the left wing that would operate the end flaps when Mary flexed her back a certain way. The metal had torn and would need to be replaced.

"What do we have here?"

Mary jumped at the sound of Roland's voice. It was one of the few times he had spoken directly to her in weeks. She turned her head to hide the tears that welled up in her eyes. He had no idea how much it meant that he was out here offering help. Mary cleared her throat, trying to knock the lump down a bit.

Mary told Roland everything that had happened with the Danes, and the bet.

Roland brushed his fingers over the wings. "Look at these poor things. It's going to take some work."

"This hinge is broken. I'm going to need to replace it. It's going to cost me more than I have to get one made."

Mary threw a screwdriver down in frustration. This time she did cry.

Mary felt Roland's arms slip around her and he hugged her. She buried her face in his arm and let loose. It was really the first time she had cried since coming to the island. She hadn't allowed herself to, but now she couldn't stop it.

Roland didn't say anything, just held her and let Mary sob herself out. Funny how something like that could be so cathartic. Mary cried away a lot of her frustration then wiped at her eyes with the backs of her hands.

"So," Roland said. "Let's see what we can do to get these things in shape. I've got a few spare parts tucked away here and there. Of course, some of them will have to be modified. These wings are much older than yours."

Mary didn't miss when he said 'yours'.

"I'm sorry for everything. I've let you down terribly."

Roland scrunched up his face. He didn't want to say it out loud, but Mary knew she had. "That's all done now. Onward and up-ward."

***

It took several days, but together the two of them finally got the wings in flying shape.

Mary slipped the wings into the harness on her back and twitched her muscles, testing the controls. They were sluggish, but there was nothing she could do about that. At least they worked.

Roland and Mary carried them up to the launch pad and she stood on the edge, feeling the thermal. She didn't think she would ever feel it again with a set of wings on her back. She had avoided coming up here all together, not wanting to be reminded of what she had lost.

"Ready?"

Mary nodded at Roland and stepped out into the thermal and dropped nearly ten feet before the wings caught the air. They were heavy, and it took several long moments before Mary could circle her way up, riding the air from the heat vent.

Mary smiled and yelled out. She was flying again. It was all she really wanted to do. Then she looked out across the open water in the direction of home, and she remembered what it was about. She needed to win this race. She needed her wings, and she needed luck on her side.

Mary dipped the tip of the nose down and screamed off over the trees.

JC Rock

Chapter Twelve

Terminal Velocity

Hope falls faster than fear. But it lands softer.

Light rain fell over the islands, a soaking drizzle that dampened Mary's spirits even more than they had been. The day had finally come for the annual games. She was nervous. Heck, she was scared shitless.

Mary had been to the games as a spectator , but here, behind the scenes, it was terrifying. Of course, Eric Dane didn't make things any easier for her. He came over just as the contestants were called for the first round.

"I hope you have been taking care of my wings."

"Don't worry," Mary told him. "They are in better shape than before the accident."

Eric shrugged, he didn't seem to care about them. "Just keep an eye peeled out on the course. You know some people try to cheat. Wouldn't want anything to happen to you."

Mary wasn't sure if he was just taunting her, or alluding to something he might do. Either way, she tried to let it bounce off her. She had racing to do.

***

Both Mary and Eric rose quickly through the levels, until it was the last two heats before the final.

Mary stood on the edge of the pad, her feet just touching the thermals that rushed up around her. Mary stepped off and the heavy wings dropped her, but she was used to it now. She worked until she was level with the other four competitors in her heat.

The five of them lined up, heading for the imaginary starting line. Mary started to pull forward of the others so tilted the nose up to scrub a little speed so that they all crossed the line at roughly the same time.

A cannon sounded in the distance, signaling it was a clean start. And they were off.

For the first part of the race Mary knew she was going to fall back. She had the heaviest wings of the bunch. But that would be an advantage for the end. The first part of the race was little more than a slalom course marked by bright red balls attached to the tops of tall poles.

Each competitor had to swoop around the outside of each balloon in succession, in the fastest time possible. The wings Mary had were heavy, unable to make very quick turns, but still she managed to keep with the other men, if just a bit back from them. Mary crossed the first marker only a few seconds back from the leader. Now it was time to shine.

Everyone headed toward the mountain, with its strong thermal vents. There were two possible paths Mary could take at that point. A shorter route, with few thermals, and a longer one.

If Mary had lighter wings, she would have taken the shorter path. Mary was familiar with the thermals on this side of the mountain, but so was everyone else. She headed for the first big thermal, angling her nose up.

Mary rode the thermal around and around, higher than most would have, but she could sense when the lift was worth it, and when it wasn't. Once the thermal began to give out, she dipped the nose down and shot from the thermal, her eyes watering from the speed. This was where the heavier wings paid off.

Mary raced from thermal to thermal. Since she had spent so much time on the first, Mary was farther behind than she should be. But that had been the strategy she worked out for this race. Mary came out of the first thermal much higher than anyone else who chose the long path, so she had more speed going into each successive thermal. She skipped over top of the second, gaining just a bit of lift before moving on to the next. She passed one flier with that move.

Each successive thermal Mary entered higher than anyone else and soon found herself neck and neck with second place. The first place flier had taken the shorter route, so it would be many more minutes before she even knew where he was.

Mary felt someone closing on her, blocking the winds she rode. She tried to drop a bit to get clear of the wash from the flier next to her, but the one coming up behind crowded too close, and she lost the wind.

Mary dropped several feet. She searched her memory for the next thermal on the course. She'd lost too much altitude, it was time to do something drastic.

Mary aimed for the base of the next thermal, nose tilted downward. Just as she reached the edge of the thermal, Mary threw the nose high into the air again and swooped straight up the thermal, bypassing the two who had caused her problems in the first place as they circled around, gaining altitude. Mary heard cheering coming from somewhere.

Mary was still in trouble though, flying nearly straight up in the thermal it was going to be hard to break out of it. Fortunately the heavier wings helped in that respect as well. The wings shuddered as she threw them straight and eased to the edge of the thermal. It scrubbed a lot of her speed, but she was able to break free and head for the next in line. She didn't know where the one who took the short path was, but at least she had passed up the others on her own path.

Mary risked a glance back and found herself several hundred feet ahead. It would have to do. She had to focus on gaining speed to be able to catch the man on the short path once the paths combined again. She skipped by the edge of next thermal and only caught half of the next one after that. She knew there was only one more thermal before the paths met again. How was she going to get speed out of it?

When Mary hit the final thermal she tilted sideways, skimming the outer edge of the thermal, gaining lift but not getting caught in the center. She lost some speed, but not as much as she would have had she had to break away from the center. Mary rode the outside of the thermal to the top and dropped out a bit early, heading around a long curve of the mountain. Then she saw him.

The one who had taken the short path was right below her, streaking along and hopping the thermals like Mary had been doing. Only difference was, Mary had the altitude. She angled her nose down toward the finishing line, planning to hop each thermal for only a second or so as she descended at a great angle.

The man in the lead glanced back and Mary saw him flinch, even from the distance. He rode much lower and needed to take a straighter line to the finish, rising each thermal longer. Mary knew she had him. He knew she had him.

When they crossed through the same thermal, he did the only thing he could at the moment. He drew close under Mary, blocking the air and stalling her out. Of course, it slowed his progress as well. Mary had to pray she had enough height to gain speed before he could ride the thermal up and out.

Mary skipped along the edge of the thermal, banking tight around the mountain toward the finish line. She could feel him draw close, but it wasn't enough to catch her. She slipped over the finish marker, with cheers following her to the landing zone. She had made it to the finals. One more race and she could have her wings back. That was, of course, if Mary beat Eric.

Chapter Thirteen

Ash and Altitude

*I burned for this. And I'd do it again just
to see the stars.*

Roland met Mary after she landed, a wide smile on his face.

"Almost there, girl," he said. "That was a heck of a race. Like nothing I've ever seen. You do that in this next race and they don't stand a chance of beating you."

Mary hoped he was right. It had been a gamble to ride that first thermal up, and even more of one to wing tip the one at the end. Mary could have lost too much speed, but it payed off.

Mary hugged Roland and thanked him for everything he had done for her. She could see in his eyes what he was thinking. He wanted her to win, but he knew that if she did, that Mary was going to leave him and Alice. There was nothing that was going to keep her there.

"Come on," he said. "Let's go get you something to drink before the final."

"I want to watch Eric's race. He needs to win, or this has all been for nothing."

Roland shrugged. "He will win. Look who he is up against."

Mary glanced at the round-board that held the names of all the competitors and their positions. Every name in the second semifinal was a crony of Eric's. No doubt there. Mary was sure Eric would win anyway, but against his own people it was a guarantee.

"A cup of hot chocolate would be wonderful. This rain has soaked right into my bones."

Roland slipped his arm around her shoulders and led her off to the contestant's cantina for hot drinks. Mary wasn't sure she could actually keep anything down, as nervous as she was, but it would be nice to get out of the rain for a bit. During the race Mary barely noticed it, now it seemed to nag at her, dripping down her back and seeping into her boots.

***

Mary heard the cannon go off in the distance. The second semi-final started. Roland looked at her, wanted to say something. That much she was sure of.

"What?"

"Your test flight... You said you had trouble breathing?"

Mary wasn't sure what he was talking about, then she remembered. During one of the quiet times after her arrest, Mary tried to make conversation with him. Mostly she did the talking as she told him about the test flight, and the things that had happened.

"Yep, blacked out for just a second two. Fortunately, I came to just in time. I guess once I got low enough for there to be enough oxygen."

"How high were you?"

"About 10,000 or so, maybe a little higher." Mary glanced at the brass altimeter on her wrist, wiped some water from the face of it.

"Ten... I don't think I have ever been that high."

Mary shrugged. "It was a little scary."

Roland nodded. "So, how do you plan to deal with that once you head for the mainland? If, you know... if you still intend to go."

Mary did. And that was something she hadn't thought about.

How was she going to breathe at such heights?

"I guess I hadn't given it much thought."

"Well, give it some," Roland said.

Mary's mind was blank. This wasn't exactly the right time for something like that: she was far too nervous for the upcoming race. She shrugged again.

"I have an idea. If you would like to hear it."

"Sure."

Roland sat back and pulled a small bag from an inner coat pocket. He pulled out what looked like a face mask, goggles and all, with a hose attached to it.

Mary's brows drew closer together. "What's that for?"

"It's for you to breathe. We attach a canister to it, one that has been modified and filled with oxygen. Maybe a pressure regulator so that when you are too high, it opens the valve and keeps a small amount of oxygen flowing."

Mary had to admit, it was a damn good idea, and she let him know it. "That's brilliant. How much does it weigh?"

Roland handed it over. "Barely anything, a few ounces. With the hose and canister, the whole apparatus will be less than two pounds."

With his talk about the canister, Mary had to broach the subject. "I'm going to need at least eight canisters to make the flight, four to a side. Do you think I will be able to get them?"

Mary didn't fancy another clandestine mission to break into the storehouse again.

"I have a friend who maybe can get them. You let me worry about that."

Since they had made up, Roland was his old self again. Still, she could see it in his eyes that he didn't want her to go, but he knew she had to at least try. For her sister.

"And I will need to come up with a way to mount them and change the directed output. I have a few ideas there."

"Maybe we could rig up something that would discard the empty canisters as well, to save that bit of weight. It might make a difference."

There was another cannon boom, and the race was over. Mary glared out the window at the round-board, waiting for them to post the results. She breathed a sigh of relief when Eric Dane was posted as first. Of course, she didn't have to wait long for him to show up and gloat some more.

"Another hour and your suffering will all be over," Eric said. "Once I beat you, you won't need to concern yourself with the wings, or flying again."

Mary didn't rise to the bait. And that upset him. His face grew red, and he stomped off, glowering over his shoulder.

"Proud of ya, girl. A year ago you woulda shortened his nose."

Mary nodded. "Look where that got me."

Roland stood, putting a hand on her shoulder. "Get some rest and dry off. This will all be over soon enough."

Roland left her sitting there holding her hot chocolate. It had grown cold.Mary set the cup down and pulled the watch from her pocket and flipped the dial, remembering she hadn't gotten her fortune for the day. As she did every time she opened the watch, Mary thought about Melvin, with his goofy little grin.

Mary flipped the dial face and pressed the button for her fortune. It spun for a moment then slowly stopped. The dial read 'Some things are best left unknown'.

Mary wasn't sure what she wanted it to say, but that wasn't it.

Mary slipped off to her assigned room to have a bit of a rest. The room had a small coal heater under the table so she turned it up to its highest setting and let it dry out her prune feet.

***

There was a knock on the door and Mary crawled out of the haze of sleep she had found herself in.

"Almost time, Mary." Roland called from outside. "Ten minutes."

Mary knuckled the sleep from her eyes and pulled her socks and boots back on. They were dry and pleasantly warm.

When Mary stepped outside she smiled. The rain had stopped, and the sun peeked out between the breaking clouds. This would only help her. The thermals would be stronger without the cooling rain. Of course, that meant they would be stronger for everyone.

Roland and Mary walked to the line. Her wings were in the carrier and Roland helped her slip them on. She released the button that would unfold the wings, and nothing happened. She heard Eric snicker beside her.

Roland quickly looked at the mechanism and did something. The wings popped open with a hiss and clicked into place.

Mary got to choose her starting position on the pad because her last time had been better than any of the others. She walked the length of the launch pad, fingers dangling in the air, feeling out the thermals. It was all about the same really, but Mary made a show of choosing a spot at the edge. At least she would start with someone on only one side of her. The others filed in according to their qualifying times. Eric was second and took the spot clear on the other end. Mary was sure he meant to take the shorter route, he had done it in each of his other races.

Mary stepped from the platform at the signal and circled her way up, followed by the others.

Once everyone was at the right altitude, they lined up as they had on the launch pad and headed for the starting line. Eric eased out by a few feet, already gaining speed as they crossed the line. Mary expected to hear the trumpeting blast to sound a false start, but instead the cannon reverberated around the trees.

Mary saw the grin on Eric's face as he pulled forward. She looked away. There was work to do.

They maintained their positions through the first few thermals. Then they reached the split point. Mary expected Eric to take the short path, but everyone kept their position.

For the first time Mary looked at the other competitors and groaned.

Each one was a friend of Eric's. Cheating wasn't allowed of course, but still there were things that could be done that only bent the rules. If they were caught doing it, they could be punished, but it rarely happened because it was so hard to catch someone doing it.

Mary tried her tactic learned from the last race and remained in the first thermal, rising it all the way to the top. It didn't work this time. Apparently, everyone had been watching. One of the fliers slipped in the thermal right under her, blocking a large portion of her lift. It was a struggle just staying aloft, let alone gaining any lift at all. She dumped out of the thermal early, dipping low to catch the next.

Eric wasn't anywhere in her sight. She knew he was the one she had to keep up with. Mary slid down toward the ground and entered the next thermal only twenty feet or so from the heat vent opening. Mary pulled the nose up as much as she thought was safe and zoomed up inside the thermal, gaining altitude just from her speed alone, then settled in and gained more and more height from the thermal rise, circling around. Mary made a counterclockwise rise instead of the normal clockwise, hopefully throwing her followers off, at least for this thermal. Mary knew she was going to have to mix it up some, to keep them guessing.

The tactic worked, for that thermal anyway, and she could ride it all the way up until it started to peter out. Mary trimmed the tail a bit and aimed for the next thermal, dipping the nose low. The pursuit came, just as she expected. She watched them, making sure they were prepping to hit the thermal, one banking from one side to spiral, the other to spiral the opposite way. Mary knew what she had to do.

She slipped through the thermal, barely touching it and racing to the next. By the time her pursuers caught on to what had happened, they were already trapped in the thermals lift and had to work to get out of it.

Mary aimed for the next thermal and caught a glimpse of Eric just exiting it. She entered the thermal halfway up. Sure, she lost some lift that way, but she had good speed to force her way to the top and out quickly.

Slowly but surely Mary caught up to Eric and was within a hundred feet, with about a quarter of the race to go. She started to lose ground to the closest pursuer behind her though, and he was right on her tail.

As Mary rode the next thermal up, her pursuer came in hot and heavy right above her, blocking her ascent. Mary had to angle away, abandoning the thermal in favor of the next. She had to scrub a lot of speed exiting, but managed to catch a break from a slight tailwind.

Mary was high enough that she skipped through the next two thermals, only skirting the very edges. She came up to the next, only feet away from Eric, so close she could almost touch him. He turned to her and grimaced, apparently surprised she was so close. Mary followed him up the thermal, employing the blocking technique that had been used on her. It worked, just a bit, the lighter wings he had kept the effect from being too dramatic.

No matter what Mary tried, she just couldn't close up the final gap between them, and there were only a few thermals left.

Only a drastic measure would get Mary the speed she needed. It could cost her the race, too.

Mary wing-tipped the next thermal, knowing it was a short one. The next one after that was a tall thermal, one she was familiar with. For a moment Mary was in the lead, but she had to climb the thermal to get her speed back up as Eric shot out of the one Mary had bypassed. He skirted the one she climbed.

Mary knew he was going to climb the next short one and then wing clip the next ones, barely hitting them for a bit of lift before heading to the finish line. If it worked, he would cross the line only a few feet up off the ground, but should have a nice lead.

Mary rode the thermal up, wincing at the appearance of Eric pulling so far ahead. At the top, she angled the nose down, hoping it would be enough. It had to be.

Mary felt the thermal give up, and she instantly turned the nose downward into a near vertical dive. It was all or nothing at this point. Even over the sound of the wind rushing quickly by her ears, she heard the crowd nearby gasp.

Mary's wing slipped through the next thermal, too strong. It pushed the left side up and threatened to drive her into the ground.

Mary fought the heavy wings with all her might, trying to keep level. She scrubbed speed. There was only one thing she could do. She allowed the turn, flipping upside down and using the momentum to right herself again.

Mary tipped the final thermal and slipped beside Eric just as they crossed the finish line. The cannon sounded. Had she won?

Mary landed heavily, shrugging the wings off and looking up at the judge's stand. After a long moment, she was marked the winner. She had done it.

"Protest," Eric yelled, running up to the judge's stand.

Mary rushed up to him. "I beat you fair and square."

The judges walked quickly up to them, thankfully pulling them apart before Mary lost her cool and punched him again.

"What is the grounds of your protest?" a judge asked.

"She missed a thermal," Eric said. "The last one."

"I did not!"

The judge held up his hand, silencing them both. They waited as another judge came running up the path from the final thermal.

"Did you see the contestants run through the thermal?" The judge leaned in, listening to the report. They conferred back and forth for a minute. Then the judge stepped forward and grabbed Mary's hand, holding it up in the air.

There was more cheering. Mary had done it.

Mary didn't want to get up into Eric's face so soon after beating him, but she needed her prize. "My wings?"

"No way. You cheated. I'm not giving them to you."

Mary heard someone clear their throat to the side. Eric's father stood there, arms crossed. He glanced at Mary. She could see the hatred in his eyes, but then he turned to Eric. "A deal is a deal. You will give the girl the wings."

For once, in all the time Mary had known him, Eric looked contrite as he shriveled back from his father's glare. "I will have them delivered to your house by the end of the day."

Chapter Fourteen

Mary, Rising

They said it was impossible. I didn't argue.
I just flew.

Roland and Mary worked tirelessly over the next few weeks modifying the wings. She knew he still had mixed feelings about her leaving, but there was nothing he could say or do that would deter her.

Somehow, Roland managed to find Mary nine canisters; eight for propulsion, and one for the breathing apparatus that he had invented. When she asked him about them, he just shook his head so she didn't push the subject. They used a pump to fill one canister with oxygen, compressing it to near the breaking point. Mary tinkered a gauge that would open a tiny valve once a certain altitude was reached. She wouldn't need it much, just after a canister burn when she was at maximum altitude.

The mounting of the four canisters on either side proved to be the most challenging thing. In the end, they decided on a system that mounted the canisters close up to the wings, allowing for the least wind resistance, and allowing the canisters to be ejected after they were empty.

Mary rigged a cable system that would blow the valves off two canisters at a time, giving her twice the power and speed. Twist the cable one way and it would fire off the valve, twist it another way and it would release the empty from the back of the magazine, allowing the next pair to drop down into place, ready to be fired when needed.

Mary wanted to leave the day she had everything finished, but it had been raining. If she was going to ensure she had the best chance, a nice sunny morning to start would do the trick.

***

The trip up to the launching pad was a long one. Mary had mixed feelings about leaving. She had to try, Beatrice needed her, and she had been away far too long. But Mary had grown to love Roland and Alice, and a few others. Not Eric; Mary wasn't going to miss Eric one bit. But if she could make it back to the mainland, then she could easily get a boat and come back to visit whenever she wanted. But first she had to get back.

Roland slipped the wings up on her back. The extra weight was noticeable, but wasn't too bad. With the full canisters, the wings weighed only a few pounds more than the ones she had used in the games.

Mary slipped her arms around Roland's waist, hugging him tight. Alice stayed back with the few people that had come to see her off. Mary could see tears in her eyes, but she was smiling at the same time. Mary scanned the small crowd, disappointed when she didn't see Hubert. Mary had hoped he would make the journey over to see her one last time, but he hadn't.

No sense putting things off. Mary stepped up to the edge of the pad.

Alice rushed up and pushed a small sack into her hand. "I made sandwiches. Just in case you get hungry."

Mary started to say thanks, but Alice quickly hugged her and then rushed off down the hill. Mary could hear her sobbing as she ran.

Mary tucked the sack into her messenger bag and slipped on the face-mask Roland had made. She adjusted the valve to draw in outsice air. It was a little uncomfortable, but she could deal with it. The goggles had blue lenses on a flip-hinge, so Mary closed them, giving everything a slight blue tint. She looked at Roland and nodded. She stepped off into the thermal. No sense delaying.

Mary rode the thermal up as high as it would take her, then slipped on to the next, and the next after that one. Mary slipped into the last thermal over land, slowly circling around as she rose beside the mountains edge. Hubert stood on a small path, waving at her.

Mary waved back. And then she was over the water.

***

Mary rode the weak thermals for nearly an hour and then came the point she had to use the first canister set. Mary angled the nose down, gathering speed before she twisted the cable to release the valve on the first set, then turned her dive into a steep climb. The directional valves Roland came up with worked and Mary had a nice steady climb. From the mask, she heard a single click, and cool air rushed in through the hose. She glanced at the altimeter. Right on 10,000 feet.

The sound of air rushing by slowed a bit and Mary felt the thrust from the canisters stop, so she leveled out and twisted the cable the other direction, expelling the empties. Mary turned her head to watch the next set drop into place as expected with a grin of satisfaction. She started a slow glide, seeking out thermals to keep the height up.

Mary wasn't sure how far she had traveled on that first canister set, dozens of miles perhaps, she really had nothing to judge by. At one point, she thought she saw a ship on the horizon and thought to fly to it and land in the water nearby. But she couldn't be sure of what she had seen in the first place, and it would have taken her off her direct route. She pressed on.

An hour or so later, Mary used the second set of canisters, shooting into the air once again. It grew harder and harder to catch a strong thermal over the water. On the island the natural vents made the thermals, out here on the water it was weather patterns that had to do the work. A cold patch of air could be the difference in making it to the mainland, or not.

Mary kept her climb at a low angle, going more for speed than altitude. When she heard the valve open for her breather mask, she leveled out, keeping only a slight climb going.

Once the second set of canisters was expended, Mary ejected them.

***

Mary rode the thermals for several hours, the sun sinking low behind her. Her back screamed in agony; she hadn't counted on the physical effort it took to make the trip. If her guess was right, she had flown about half-way to the mainland, though she really had no idea how far it was. She scanned the water for boats, or any indication of where she was, but nothing came to her.

As the sun dipped below the horizon, Mary fired off another set of canisters. The thermals grew weaker as night fell. When the canisters expended themselves, Mary twisted the cable. Nothing happened. One canister slipped out, but the other stayed firmly in place, cocked at an odd angle.

Mary reached back, trying to jar the canister loose, but she could barely reach the edge. She could only get the edges of her fingernails on the canister. Each time she reached back, the nose dipped down from her movements. Mary regained her momentum and kept flying forward. She still had a while before she would have to use the last set. Hopefully she would be within sight of land before that happened.

Catching thermals came a bit easier for a while, and once, Mary even passed over a few specks of island. Uninhabited, but at least she was able to catch a good thermal off of them. Mary flew like that for a couple of hours and knew it would soon be time to hit the next set of canisters. She needed to do something.

The canister that held Mary's oxygen was at her belt, clipped on with a small hook. She slipped the hook loose and reached back but the hose wasn't long enough. She slipped the hose free and used the butt of the canister to push at the one that was jammed. After several minutes Mary was finally able to push it free. As it shot out of the magazine, Mary dropped the air canister. Her fingers fumbled with it, almost catching it, but then it was lost, spiraling down to the black ocean.

Mary pulled the useless mask off and dropped it away. She knew it was going to be interesting on the next canister burn.

Mary was only a hundred feet or so off the ocean so it was time again. The weak thermals in the ocean wouldn't lift her enough without help. Mary fired the last set of canisters and rose quickly, keeping her ascent tight. There was no way she would be able to climb straight up, but still kept the angle fairly large.

Mary glanced at the tiny gauge on her wrist; at 20,000 feet, she saw dark cliffs and lights in the distance. The mainland. But from this height she could tell she still had miles and miles to go. Mary tried to do the math in her head, but she couldn't think straight. Her vision grew black at the edges and she was forced to level out. The canisters burned a minute longer, then stopped. That was it.

Last chance to make it. Perhaps this close to land she would be able to find a boat.

Mary fought the urge to throw up. She was light-headed and found it a chore to breathe normally. It was like she had to work twice as hard to get the air needed.

Mary shivered in the cold. She thought about how she should have brought a coat with her, but that would have just weighed her down even more.

Mary ejected the spent canisters and set in for a long glide in the dark with her teeth chattering. At one point she thought she saw lights on the water, but couldn't be sure. The thermals at this height were few and far between, and difficult to find.

Mary drifted along, the wind burning through her watery eyes. Her ears were raw from the cold. Still, the lights of the mainland drew closer and closer.

Three hours passed, and then four. Mary was frozen to the bone. She couldn't feel her feet at all and her fingers were numb blocks of ice, even in the gloves she wore.

Mary flew over a few small islands, but there didn't appear to be any lights, so she bypassed them and headed on until she slipped over the outer edge of the mainland.

Mary smiled to herself. Now she just needed to find a spot she could land near a town. She had no idea where she was, or if this was even England. But at this point it didn't even matter.

The dark shadows of buildings appeared on the horizon, with a few lights in windows. Her altitude had dropped to just over a thousand feet so she tilted the nose down and aimed for the middle of the town and a small park that was surrounded by street lamps.

Mary tried getting her feet out under her to land, but she was too weak and ended up swooping down over the land and tilting one wing tip over until it could touch the ground. The tip dug in and flung her around. With frozen fingers, she slipped the release on the harness and went tumbling along the wet grass, thumping heavily against a tree.

Mary lay there on the grass, shivering and faint. A few people must have seen her descent and were closing in. She had made it somewhere at least. But she knew her journey still wasn't over; Beatrice was waiting.

Afterword

Every story ends.
Sometimes it ends quietly—so quietly, you don't realize it until the moment is already gone.

That's what I tried to capture here. Not explosions, not revelations, but the slow unravelings. The quiet disconnections. The echo left behind when something small, but deeply personal, comes to a close.

Several of the stories in this collection originally appeared in anthologies published by Corrugated Sky Publishing, a small press that is now (sadly) defunct. I'm grateful they found a first home there—and even more grateful to share them again now, together.

None of these stories were meant to be loud.
They were meant to be *true*.

I hope something in them stayed with you.
A feeling. A line. A silence you recognized.

If so—thank you.
That's all a writer ever hopes for.

— JC Rock

About the Author

JC Rock writes quiet stories about loud feelings—the kind that sneak up on you and stay long after the page turns. He lives full-time in a converted school bus, where there's just enough room for a ukulele, a stack of half-finished drawings, and an unapologetically large spice rack.

When he's not writing, he's probably cooking something slow, reading something strange, or imagining how the world ends in small, beautiful ways.

This is his first collection.